"Ah, the well-behaved Miss Fenton."

The earl's voice was laced with pain and sarcasm.

Serena, whose remorse had risen as they assisted the earl to the sofa, felt as if she'd been slapped. Stiffening, she said, "My apologies, my lord. If you had not startled me, I would never have lost my grip."

"A proper female would never have been up a tree!" he roared back.

"I suppose I should sit in the parlour all day doing needlepoint?" she demanded.

"That's what normal females do!"

After a short, stunned silence, Serena replied with as much dignity as she could muster. "Then, my lord, I have no desire to be either proper or normal."

Lord Granville gingerly moved his wrist propped on a pillow. A shaft of pain made his words twice as sharp.

"Then, my dear Miss Fenton, you have nothing to fear, for I assure you that you are in no danger of becoming either!"

CUPID AND THE VICAR

JUDITH STAFFORD

Harlequin Books

TORONTO • NEW YORK • LONDON
AMSTERDAM • PARIS • SYDNEY • HAMBURG
STOCKHOLM • ATHENS • TOKYO • MILAN

Published November 1991

ISBN 0-373-31162-1

CUPID AND THE VICAR

PROLOGUE

THE YOUNG VICAR faced the newly anointed earl. The fact that he owed his advantageous position to the man, in addition to their long-standing friendship, made the reason for this conversation difficult.

"What is it, Daniel?" Lord Granville asked, keenly aware of a vast number of additional demands on his time.

"I wanted to discuss a matter of great concern which may affect my future with you."

"You are not happy with the appointment?"

"No, of course not. I mean, I am delighted; the people of this parish have been warmly receptive, and...and I am very pleased with the work." He paused, trying to consider the proper phrasing which would best describe his problem.

"What is it then, man? You know I shall assist you in whatever way possible, but I am in the process of making arrangements to take Patty to London for her first Season, and the entire household is at sixes and sevens."

Daniel Fenton's heart sank. His friend had made reference to the very subject which concerned him. "You are going to take Patty to London?"

"Yes, it is important she marry properly. As an earl's sister, she can expect a much better marriage than when she was merely a lowly lieutenant's sister."

"And you feel that to marry well is... is important to Patty?"

"She is too young to understand where her duty lies, but I know mine."

"But what if she chooses someone who is not of a rank equal to yours?" Daniel asked carefully.

"Patty will do as I bid her. She knows I have her best interest at heart."

"But is not Patty's own happiness more important than rank and fortune?"

"I have no intention of forcing Patty to make an unhappy marriage, Daniel, but she has suffered enough poverty. Now that her rank has been elevated, I want her to enjoy the better things in life."

Though Daniel's heart shrivelled, he continued to smile, albeit stiffly. "I'm sure you will do your best for her happiness. I wish you both well."

"Thank you. Now, what is of such concern to you?"

"Me? Nothing of significance. In fact, I shall let you attend to your pressing business and speak to you of it later."

"But I shall be leaving within the week. Do not leave it too late," Marcus warned, his mind already turning to the numerous tasks he had yet to complete.

Daniel only smiled and turned to go, muttering to himself, "I believe I have already done so."

CHAPTER ONE

"DANIEL, IT IS GOOD to see you. I meant to call at the vicarage this afternoon." The two men shook hands with the ease that bespoke an enduring friendship.

"Word travelled through the parish that you had returned. How was the London Season?" enquired Daniel gently of his host.

"Much the same as last year. Patty refused all marriage proposals and returned home with me."

Startled, the young man felt his cheeks flush, even as he strove to suppress the rush of pleasure the words afforded him. "I would never presume to ask about Miss Browne's—"

"Forgive my frankness, Daniel, but you know I do not stand on ceremony with you."

With a sigh, the young man replied, "I know, Marcus, and that is the reason for my call. I am hoping to avail myself further of your goodness to me."

The dark man seated behind the desk smiled grimly. It was not often he was accused of goodness. The man before him was a good man. He was also independent. Marcus wondered what could be so serious that Daniel would actually solicit his help.

"You have always extended your hospitality to me in spite of our difference in rank. I have come to ask that your graciousness be extended to my sister."

"Your sister?"

"Yes, my youngest sister is coming to live with me." Daniel paused and bit his bottom lip. His friend waited patiently. "I wish to find a husband for my sister," he burst out, as if admitting a shameful thing.

Marcus raised one eyebrow but again waited for his friend to continue.

"I hoped you would assist me. Perhaps there is a local squire or a worthy widower you might be able to introduce to her. Her birth is good, but her portion is small."

With an inward groan, Marcus smiled benevolently. "Of course, Daniel. I shall do my best to assist you. And any invitation to you will include your sister from now on."

Daniel stood, a grateful smile on his face. "Thank you, Marcus." He extended his hand once more before withdrawing.

Marcus sat back down at his desk, a frown on his brow. He had just spent a great deal of time and money trying to marry off his sister Cleopatra with a remarkable lack of success. Now he was expected to find a husband for Daniel's sister, as well.

Daniel slipped from the big house, guilt written all over his face. He was uncomfortably aware of the impropriety of asking Marcus for his assistance, especially since he had an ulterior motive. Though as far as he knew, the Church had placed no prohibitions on matchmaking, Daniel still did not feel at ease. A vicar should not take on the role of Cupid.

MISS CLEOPATRA BROWNE pulled her wool cloak closer around her diminutive but well-rounded form. She could have called out her brother's carriage for her errand, but she hoped the walk would help her grow more slender, like the other young women she'd met in London. Secretly she feared it was a useless task, since she had never been slender in her life.

The sharp October wind ruffled the cheesecloth covering her basket. Tucking it in, she patted the lump underneath. She hoped Daniel would like her new receipt for pumpkin bread. It at least provided her with a good excuse for calling on him. How she had missed his gentle humour, his smile, during the long months in London. If only Marcus would not insist on parading her before the ton. She had no desire to marry one of those dandies, who were interested only in their shirt points or cravats.

Life had been much easier before her brother inherited his title. Of course she'd not had as many pretty dresses or as many servants. But his elevation also brought unwanted complications to her life.

Reaching the vicarage, she rapped upon the door. When it was swung open by Mrs. Washburn, the vicarage housekeeper, she asked, "Is Mr. Fenton in this afternoon?"

"Yes, he is, Miss Browne. You come right in out of that cold wind. It's good to see you back from London."

"Thank you, Mrs. Washburn. I'm glad to be back. How is everyone?"

"Fine, fine. The cat had a litter of kittens last week, and little Tommy Black broke his arm when he fell out of a tree."

"Oh, dear. The doctor attended him?"

"Yes'm," the woman assured her as she led the way to Mr. Fenton's study. Knocking on the door, as she opened it she announced the caller. "Mr. Fenton, Miss Browne is here."

Cleopatra's cheeks glowed crimson as the tall gentleman jumped to his feet. How good it was to see him. "Daniel, we have returned. I wished to show you what I learned while I was away," she said gaily, holding her basket out to him as Mrs. Washburn left, pulling the door to behind her.

Daniel Fenton swallowed the lump in his throat. He had thought himself prepared for Patty's return, but the rush of happiness which filled him when he saw her left him quite speechless.

"Won't you even look at what I have prepared?" she prompted when he did not move.

"Yes, of course, Miss Browne," he replied stiffly and reached to take the basket from her.

Cleopatra withdrew her basket from his reach and stamped her foot. "Daniel! Have I been gone so long that we have become strangers?"

"Of—of course not! But I should not...I am the vicar and you are the sister of an earl."

"Oh, pooh! We are friends, Daniel. I refuse to be relegated to Miss Browne."

"Very well, Patty, as long as we are not in company. Now, what have you brought in your basket?"

She took his hand and led him over to the horsehair sofa. "I discovered a new receipt for pumpkin bread and I baked some for you. Will you not try it?"

Daniel received the fragrant slice of bread from her small hand. With a smile of pleasure, he took a bite and chewed it deliberately. "Excellent, Patty, as always. Will you share your new receipt with the women in our parish? It should make a nice addition to tea." In truth, in her pale blue muslin gown, he thought she was more tempting than her pumpkin bread.

"Of course, Daniel. Have the classes continued through the summer?"

He shook his head. "I'm afraid not. There is no one willing to donate the time and patience which you give to teach the women how to prepare nourishing meals." One of Daniel's most rewarding projects was a class for the women living on Marcus's estate and the surrounding ones, teaching them better ways to prepare food and care for their families. When she was in residence, Patty always assisted him.

"I don't see why Marcus insists that I go to London for the Season. It disrupts everything."

Daniel smiled at her irritation, but he avoided her eyes. "It is only right that you take your proper place in Society." After a pause, he added, "Besides, now that my sister is coming to live with me, I'll have assistance year-round."

Cleopatra's eyes grew wide. "Your sister? She's coming here to live? I—I thought she was married."

"My older sister, Mildred, is married with several children. But Serena, my younger sister, is not. She has been residing with Mildred, but...well, Mildred is the managing sort, and Serena swears she is driving her to distraction."

"I see." Cleopatra hoped her disappointment didn't show. She had relied on Daniel's need of a helpmeet to prompt him to offer her marriage even if she herself could not tempt him to do so. Now, with his sister coming to live with him, there would be no need to wed.

"I hope you and Serena will become friends, Patty. She will need female companionship. I realize, of course, that she is only a vicar's sister—"

"Don't be absurd, Daniel. Of course I shall befriend your sister. Is she very much like you?"

Relieved that Patty's voice had returned to normal, he laughed. "No, Serena and I are not alike. Her hair is red and she has a temper to match it. I suspect she tried Mildred's patience as much as Mildred tried hers."

They sat in silence, each thinking of the young woman who would soon arrive upon Daniel's doorstep. Finally, because in the past two years Patty had become his confidante, Daniel said, "I must confess I hope Serena will not remain with me long."

Patty's heart flickered with hope, but she remained cautious. "What do you mean, Daniel?"

"I wish to find a husband for Serena. I—I asked Marcus to assist me," he added, watching Cleopatra out of the corner of his eye.

"Marcus?" she asked, her spirits reviving at the thought of Daniel's plans. "What assistance would Marcus be able to give you?"

"I asked him to invite Serena to your parties and to keep an eye out for a worthy widower or a local squire who would not require a large dowry."

"Marcus may not be of much assistance, but I shall help you. We must put our heads together and think of any eligible young men in the parish."

"I have tried, but I can only think of Mr. Jenkins."

Cleopatra stifled her giggle by clapping her hands to her lips. "Daniel! You are being absurd."

Since it had been his intent to elicit her delightful gurgle of laughter, he only smiled in return. Mr. Jenkins, in his sixtieth year and bedridden, might also have laughed if he'd heard the vicar's words.

"I know!" Cleopatra exclaimed, her eyes rounded in excitement. "Marcus!"

The expression in his eyes showed caution as Daniel questioned her. "Marcus? What do you mean?"

"Marcus is available. And if he were to marry, perhaps it would soften his hard heart." Her animated face turned sombre. "I don't think Marcus is very happy, Daniel. Could Serena bring him joy?"

"Serena could bring laughter and warmth to anyone." Cleopatra felt a decided twinge of jealousy until Daniel added, "She is like you in that respect."

She blushed at his compliment. Sometimes, as now, she felt sure Daniel cared for her, though he never gave any indication of his feelings. With a tremulous smile, she said, "Then, I believe we should persuade Marcus to marry Serena."

"She has a small dowry," Daniel warned, his gaze lingering lovingly on Cleopatra's glowing cheeks. He felt as if the sun, having been absent all summer, had returned to the vicarage once more.

"That does not matter. Marcus is quite rich, you know, in spite of what Auggie says." Augustus, Marcus's younger brother, was constantly short of funds and his pleas for a larger allowance fell on deaf ears.

"Marcus is my friend," Daniel added, without saying why that fact should alter Cleopatra's thoughts.

"All the more reason to encourage a romance," she said emphatically, suddenly discovering several possible benefits from such a match. "Then you would become a member of our family!" And she would have more opportunities to encourage his interest in her direction.

"Marcus may not take kindly to your idea. After all, I'm sure he's had many opportunities to marry, if that is his desire."

"Yes, and every one of the ladies concerned is more interested in his purse than his person," Patty assured him vehemently.

Before Daniel could respond, the door swung open to reveal Lord Granville, his brow furrowed in discontent.

"Marcus!" Patty shrieked, jumping up guiltily. "You—you startled us."

"Why did you not come in the carriage as a well brought up young lady would have done? Must you make yourself the object of gossip?"

"Good day, Lord Granville," Daniel said, his voice quiet but stern, as he stood. Marcus was his friend and generous to a fault to his people, but with his brother and sister, it seemed to Daniel, he searched for fault rather than good.

"Daniel," Marcus acknowledged, his frown still concentrated on his sister.

"Marcus, there is nothing amiss in my walking to the vicarage. We are no longer in London where I must be constrained and hemmed in." Patty drew herself up to her full height, small though she was, and raised her chin as she awaited her brother's response.

"There are gossips even in the country. A reputation for being hoydenish will follow you back to London, and you will never obtain a husband."

Daniel stood with his head bent. He might love Patty, but he comprehended her brother's desire that she assume her rightful place in Society.

Marcus looked at his friend, then turned back to his sister. "This discussion should be carried on in privacy, Patty."

"I have no secrets from Daniel," Patty protested, backing up until she was immediately in front of the vicar.

"That is probably true," Marcus replied, rueful laughter rumbling in his chest, "but Daniel might prefer that you did."

Though colour flooded Daniel's cheeks, he remained silent. Patty, relieved to see her brother's sense of humour revived, grinned. "Daniel is my friend. He does not mind."

Marcus's expression took on a more serious cast. "Even so, my dear, your deportment is a serious matter. A young woman's reputation is not to be treated lightly. At the least, you should have been accompanied by your maid." As Patty started to speak, he held up his hand and added, "And you should not confer behind closed doors with the vicar." He spared his friend a glance of apology, but Daniel's head was bent.

Patty, however, was infuriated. "Marcus! You may say what you will about me, but how dare you suggest, even for a moment, that Daniel would be dishonourable! He is—"

"Your brother is quite correct, Miss Browne," Daniel said, his eyes bleak as he interrupted. "I am at fault. It will not happen again, Lord Granville."

"Daniel—" Marcus began, alarmed at his friend's reaction when he had intended his stricture for his sister. However, voices out of doors and the squeak of ungreased wheels caused all three to turn to the window.

The heavy wagon drawn to a standstill was well known to the village. It was owned by Willy Dempster, a ne'er-do-well who took jobs hauling heavy loads in the neighbourhood. Seated up beside the man was a female form completely hidden in a navy blue wool cloak.

As they watched, the female swung herself down from the high perch, offering an immodest view of her trim ankles and one rounded calf clad in a white stocking. Once on the ground, she called back to the driver, "Thank you for your kindness, Mr. Dempster. I'll be sure to tell my brother of your assistance to me."

"Aye, my girl, you be sure to do that," the man replied with a coarse laugh before slapping the reins on the rumps of his mule team.

Daniel noted the frown of disapproval on Marcus's face even as he rushed out of the study to greet his sister. It was not an auspicious beginning.

Unaware that the others were following in his wake, he opened the front door and stepped outside. "Serena!"

With a squeal of delight, Serena picked up the skirt of her lilac wool gown and raced across the short distance to throw her arms around her brother in abandoned joy.

The two members of the Browne family were surprised by this unprecedented display of emotion, Marcus in particular. Had he not just been preaching ladylike behaviour to his sister? How, then, was he to react to this unacceptable hoyden? And why should it matter that the vibrant face topped by dark red hair, revealed as the hood fell back, was filled with love and happiness?

The young lady opened her eyes, exposing jewel-like green orbs, as unusual as the rest of her appearance, and discovered an audience. "Oh, hello," she said with a wide smile. Withdrawing from her brother's embrace, she extended a hand. "You must be friends of Daniel's. I'm Serena."

In spite of an impulse to smile back at her, Marcus executed an abbreviated bow, his brows drawn down in censure.

Serena took exception to his greeting, but Daniel rushed to interrupt any response she might make.

"Yes, Serena, this is Lord Granville, who graciously gave me my living, and his sister, Miss Browne."

The warning implicit in her brother's introduction warred with Serena's reaction to the disapproval of the man's face. After all, she'd been living with constant condemnation in the person of her older sister for the past three years. All warmth was erased from her face, and she nodded coldly with all the formality of a high-born dowager.

Cleopatra, seeing her dream of uniting the two families dissolve, stepped in front of Marcus, a warm smile on her face. "Hello, Miss Fenton. I'm delighted to make your acquaintance."

Serena responded to her warmth as a flower does to the sun. "Thank you. Do you reside in the neighbourhood?"

"Oh, yes, just over the hill. It will be nice to have someone near to me in age close by."

Serena's eyes rested briefly on the stern-faced man standing behind the gracious young woman before she replied, "And I shall no doubt enjoy visiting with *you*."

"Come, Patty, we must leave the vicar to welcome his sister properly. Dan—"

"Patty? What an unusual name!" Serena exclaimed.

"It is what my brothers call me. I am actually named Cleopatra," Patty explained ruefully, prepared for the amusement her name always elicited because of her short, wholesome appearance.

Being a kind young woman, Serena hid any laughter and simply replied, "And I am Serena." Their friendship was sealed at that moment, and as far as Cleopatra was concerned, so was her brother's fate.

Daniel bade goodbye to the Brownes and steered his beloved sister indoors. "Why did you not arrive in Mildred's coach? Surely you cannot have travelled by the common stage?"

"Mildred offered her coach but I refused," Serena explained, an angry glint returning to her green eyes.

"Why?"

Serena turned away to avoid her brother's eyes. "We had a disagreement."

"And whenever did you not?" he asked with a quiet chuckle.

"Oh, Daniel," Serena wailed, flinging herself once again into her brother's arms. "I have missed you so! Mildred never sees the humour in anything."

Daniel patted her, feeling more like her father than her brother.

Pulling back, Serena shifted her eyes away from her brother's regard. "She—she wanted me to accept Mr. Peabody's offer of matrimony."

"Who is Mr. Peabody?"

"He is a friend of Ned's," Serena exlained bitterly, naming her brother-in-law, "with detestable looks and pawing hands."

"Did he harm you?" Daniel snapped, unusual fire in his tones.

Appeased by her brother's concern, Serena leaned back against him with a sigh of relief. "No, but I could not bring myself to accept him. You are not angry with me?"

"No, my dear," Daniel assured her, hugging her close. "Mildred seems happy with the road she has taken, but I would choose differently for you."

"Oh, Daniel, I do not think marriage is the thing for me. I shall be content to assist you in your work."

Daniel sighed. "I would like to see you happily settled, my dear."

"With someone like the gentleman I just met?" Serena suggested, scorn in her voice. "I would wither and die if forced to live with his constant disapproval. Find me someone like yourself, dear Daniel, and I will consider matrimony. Until then, I shall remain at your side."

"Very well, Serena." It seemed to Daniel that his attempt to play Cupid had got off to a rather bad start.

CHAPTER TWO

THE SHORT RIDE in the Earl of Granville's carriage to his home was conducted in silence. Cleopatra stole several glances at her brother, but his glowering expression did not encourage conversation.

The carriage came to a halt in front of the wide sweep of stairs leading to the entrance to the Palladian mansion, and several servants in royal blue livery ran down the steps to open the door and assist Cleopatra to alight.

"Now, that's the proper way a young lady should descend from a vehicle," Lord Granville muttered as he followed his sister up the stairs.

Should a young lady simply remain in the vehicle until someone comes to assist her? Cleopatra wondered. Serena might have had a long wait for Willy Dempster to realize he was supposed to hand her down. She said nothing, but she was delighted to know that her brother's thoughts were lingering on Miss Fenton, even if it were to criticize.

As they crossed the threshold, Marcus's deep voice interrupted her musings. "Patty, I believe we must talk in my study."

"Oh, Marcus, I promise to be on my best behaviour. *Must* you reprimand me?"

"No, that is not—"

"My lord." The august tones of Lawrence, the Earl of Granville's butler since before the present earl was born, interrupted.

"Yes, Lawrence?" Marcus asked, but he took the precaution of grasping hold of Cleopatra's arm to prevent her from escaping.

"Mr. Browne has arrived," the butler announced gloomily. Cleopatra had yet to witness a smile upon his face, particularly on the occasion of the arrival of one of the Brownes.

"Auggie?" she enquired. "Where is he?"

"I believe Mr. Browne has ascended to his chamber, Miss Browne."

Patty felt an urge to stick out her tongue at the starched-up butler, but she didn't want to add to the length of the discussion she and Marcus would have. "Don't you want to see Auggie, Marcus?"

"Not particularly," he replied, his lips twisting into a grimace. "If he has retired to the country now, there must be a problem he cannot solve, and I do not look forward to learning of it."

"Oh, pooh! What a stick-in-the-mud you've become!"

Marcus's lips tightened. "I believe we shall retire to my study now, Cleopatra."

He rarely called her by her full name unless he was truly irritated with her. Sighing, she nodded and walked alongside him down the wide entry hall to a door almost hidden behind the curving staircase.

Hoping to forestall a lecture, Cleopatra protested as soon as she was seated, "Truly, Marcus, I don't think my strolling to the vicarage was so terrible."

"I know you do not," he replied in a gentle voice that caused Cleopatra to sit up and stare at him. When she was a child, her brother had been her idol, a kind and loving young man. It was only when he inherited the title and consequently felt he had to maintain certain standards that they had grown apart.

"What do you mean?"

"Patty... Patty, what I am about to say is difficult. You must know that I wish only your happiness."

"Marcus, please, it was not such a serious offence," Cleopatra protested.

"I am not speaking of your walk to the vicarage. Or rather, I am, but not because you went unescorted. I—I know why you refused the offers you received in London." He stood behind his desk, carefully avoiding his sister's gaze.

"I told you why I refused them. I could not care for any of them, and you promised me I did not have to marry unless my heart was... was attached." She kept her chin up but her cheeks were bright red.

Marcus moved around the desk and pulled another chair beside Cleopatra's. He sat down and took her hand in his. "Child, I know that the object of your affections is Daniel." As his sister opened her mouth to speak, he hurried on. "I have no objection to Daniel. He is a fine man, one of the best I know."

"Then why are you unhappy with me?"

"Because you have given Daniel every opportunity to demonstrate his feelings, but he has not done so. I would not have you make a spectacle of yourself chasing after him. Nor would I wish Daniel to be made uncomfortable owing to your pursuit."

"He—he *has* shown that he cares for me," Cleopatra protested, fighting back the tears which filled her eyes. "Just today, he—he was so happy to see me."

Marcus's hand tightened on Cleopatra's. "I'm sure he was, Patty, but you cannot spend all your life waiting for him to discover your love for him. If you do not marry soon, you will be considered on the shelf."

A solitary tear escaped from each of her pale blue eyes and sizzled down her heated cheeks. "I can marry no other when my heart belongs to Daniel."

"Then we are at *point non plus,* are we not?" he questioned gently. "Perhaps we should employ the art of compromise, child."

She gave a dainty sniff and looked up at her brother. "How so?"

"Suppose I allow you the time until the next Season begins to bring Daniel up to scratch." He caught his sister's surprised stare. "A vulgar term, I know, but in Daniel's case singularly appropriate."

"And . . . and if he does not offer for me?"

"Then you return to London and accept one of the proposals you will no doubt receive."

The bleak expression in his sister's eyes made Marcus feel the veriest beast, but he truly had her best interests at heart. He did not want her to turn into a lonely old woman, waiting for the one man who did not want her.

"V-very well, Marcus," Cleopatra agreed, feeling she had no alternative. But determination welled up within her. And the beginning of a plan was born at that moment. "But *you* must make me a promise, also."

Marcus frowned, his black brows almost touching above his vivid blue eyes. "And what is that?"

"You must promise to assist me if I have need of you. Because I warn you that I shall let no opportunity go by to convince Daniel that I am the perfect wife for him."

"I will not have you cause talk, Patty. You must operate within the laws of Society."

"I promise."

With a sigh, he nodded. "Very well, I promise, though I cannot feel easy about conspiring against Daniel."

Cleopatra, in the spirit of Miss Fenton, threw her arms around her brother's neck, something she had not done in some years. "Thank you, Marcus!"

"Here now, what's the to-do?" a startled young voice called from the door. A younger, less powerful version of Marcus stood in the doorway, staring at the other two members of his family.

"Auggie!" Cleopatra called, jumping from her chair and abandoning one brother for the other.

Augustus Browne returned his sister's hug in surprise. With one arm still round her, he looked suspiciously at his brother. "Been raking her over the coals, have you?"

Marcus stood and walked over to his desk, not answering his brother's accusation.

"Of course he has not," Cleopatra protested.

"Well, something must be up. You haven't greeted me with such enthusiasm since you were six and I gave you that puppy."

"She's been taking lessons of deportment from a new acquaintance," Marcus said drily before Cleopatra could respond.

"Marcus! How can you criticize Miss Fenton for being pleased to see her brother?"

"Miss Fenton?" August asked, his eyes darting back and forth between his siblings.

"Mr. Fenton's sister." When her brother continued to stare at her, she added, "Mr. Fenton is the vicar, remember?"

"What's that got to say to anything?"

"His sister arrived today and...and Marcus did not approve of her deportment."

"I see," Augustus said, sending a bitter look his brother's way. "He's no longer satisfied to criticize *our* behaviour, but must now survey the neighbourhood looking for more victims."

Cleopatra cast a troubled glance between her two brothers. Somehow, since Marcus inherited the title, they had all grown further apart. She felt the need to talk to Daniel about their estrangement.

"And to what do we owe the pleasure of your company, little brother?" Marcus asked in hardened tones.

Augustus's bitterness was replaced by a swiftly concealed dismay. "Just thought I'd see how Patty was going on. Take a break from Town life. That's all. Ain't I welcome in your demmed palace?" he almost shouted.

"Remember that you are supposed to be a gentleman, Augustus," Marcus replied, indicating his sister with his eyes.

"I didn't offend Patty, did I, love?"

Caught between her two brothers, Cleopatra sought a peaceful solution. "Come along, Auggie, and leave Marcus in peace. He has had enough to

deal with today, and we only just arrived ourselves." With a smile at her older brother's look of
surprise, she shoved Augustus out the door of the
study and pulled it to behind her.

"You defending him now?" Augustus demanded, outraged at what he perceived as his sister's betrayal.

"I think we may have judged Marcus too harshly,
Auggie. His has not been an easy road the past two
years."

"Ha! Give me unlimited wealth, three estates and
all the ladies chasing after me, and *I'd* be happy."

Cleopatra couldn't hold back a smile, but she felt
much older than Augustus, who numbered four
years beyond her twenty. "I know it seems that
should be so, Auggie, but a great number of responsibilities come with such things, and Marcus wasn't
raised to assume them. Who would have imagined
that Marcus, as a distant cousin of the former earl,
would become Lord Granville."

"Not me. But that don't mean he should vent his
spleen on his only relatives. He's been deuced unpleasant." Augustus frowned and rammed his fists
into his pockets.

"Are you in difficulties again?"

Augustus shot a quick glance at his sister's anxious face and then looked away. "Of course not!
Can't a fellow wish to see his family without everyone thinking he's done something wrong?"

While Cleopatra had her own ideas about Augustus's visit, it did not seem to be a good time to question him further. "I am glad you have come," she said simply, surprising her brother with another hug. Marcus was right: she had learned something from Miss Fenton already.

THE NEXT MORNING, a footman in royal blue livery delivered a note to the vicarage.

"A message from the big house," Mrs. Washburn announced, but instead of handing the note to the vicar who had extended his hand, she added, "For Miss Serena."

The young lady looked up in surprise. "For me?"

Under her brother's watchful eye, she read the note. "Miss Browne is inviting me for a drive about the area to familiarize myself with my new home. Shall I accept, Daniel?"

"Absolutely, my dear," Daniel assured, pleased. "That is very kind of Patty—I mean, Miss Browne."

Though Serena noted her brother's red-faced confusion, she only said, "Yes, it is. Excuse me while I reply to her invitation. Is the man waiting for a response, Mrs. Washburn?"

"Yes'm, he is. I'll give him a cup o' tea whilst you pen your note."

CLEOPATRA SAT SEDATELY in the barouche and sent a footman to the door to alert Miss Fenton of her arrival. Marcus would have been proud of her, she thought, a small smile playing over her generous lips. *She* would have preferred going to the door herself in the hope of seeing Daniel, but she was making a concerted effort to please Marcus.

The sight of Serena Fenton filled Cleopatra with envy. The graceful, slender figure was clothed in a green wool walking dress with a black velvet cloak lined in matching green silk. Her auburn hair peeked from beneath her stylish bonnet topped with two green plumes. She presented a wonderfully vibrant picture as she entered the carriage.

"Good morning, Miss Browne. I so much appreciate your invitation."

And she had good manners, as well, thought Patty, musing that Marcus would approve of her guest today as much as he had not yesterday.

"I am delighted to accompany you, Miss Fenton. I hope to further our acquaintance because Daniel—Mr. Fenton—is a particular friend of our family as well as being our vicar. You are aware that he and Marcus were schoolmates?"

"Yes, I believe he did mention that in his letter when he received the appointment. It was kind of your brother to remember him."

Cleopatra turned her head towards Serena and, though smiling, said seriously, "That time was difficult for Marcus, and Daniel gave him great comfort and support in those early months."

At Serena's inquisitive look, Cleopatra explained, "The sixth Earl of Granville was a distant cousin with two sons of his own. Marcus did not expect to inherit. But the younger son died of smallpox. Then, a little over two years ago, the older boy fell from his horse, his head striking a rock. When they carried his body back to the house, his father fell over dead from shock." She paused to sigh. "Poor Marcus was on the Continent serving the Duke of Wellington. It was a great shock to him, as well."

"It must have been," Serena murmured.

"Here is the village up ahead," Cleopatra said, gesturing to the collection of shops and houses clustered about the small road.

Serena turned her head to look at the various points of interest, but she studied her companion frequently. The relationship between this young woman and her brother interested her.

"There is the shop of the local modiste, but your wardrobe is far superior to her skills."

"Thank you," Serena replied with a wry twist of her cupid's-bow lips. "My sister was most generous in that regard."

"She resides in London?"

"Yes, though on the outskirts of Society. I lived for the past three years with her."

"Then we were in London these past two years at the same time!" Cleopatra exclaimed. "I wish I had known."

"We do not move in the same circles," Serena assured her briefly.

"Were you miserable, also?" Cleopatra asked in a whisper.

Serena swung her gaze sharply to her companion. She did not think she had given away her feelings.

Fearing she had offended her guest, Cleopatra said, "I am sorry. Daniel said...that is..."

Serena, with her eyes fixed on the driver of the carriage, said, "Could we not stop and look in the window of that shop? I—I might purchase a book for my brother."

"Yes, of course," Cleopatra said stiffly, smarting from Miss Fenton's snub.

The footman assisted them down from the carriage and the young ladies strolled over to stare in the shop window of the local bookseller.

"Forgive me, but I did not think we should discuss such matters before the servants," Serena whispered, surprising her companion.

"Oh! I thought...I thought I had offended you. But, you see, Daniel informed me you were unhappy with your sister. I thought perhaps it was because you hated the Season as much as I."

"I do not think we experienced the same Season," Serena said with a wry chuckle. "My Season consisted of several dull card parties attended by wealthy Cits and a few nights in attendance at the theatre."

"That does not sound like a proper Season. Why did you not attend the balls? Your wardrobe must have been adequate if your sister was generous."

"It was not my wardrobe that was inadequate, but my connections." With a sigh, Serena explained, "Our sister, Mildred, married a wealthy man. But he owns wool factories in the North. He offered for my sister because he hoped for a social entrée. Mildred boasted of her connections in the ton. Once they were married, Ned discovered my sister was not well received because of her disagreeableness. And once she was married to a merchant, they were invited to only the least exclusive events."

Cleopatra took her companion's arm and they strolled along the street. "Are they happily married?"

"I do not see how anyone could be happily married to that man. He is a dullard and obsessed with finances. He is resentful of Mildred's social failures. I think he had hoped to be knighted."

"How dismal it must have been for you."

"Yes. I avoided the man as much as possible. His gaze would remain on me if we were in the same room. But the situation grew even worse when his friend decided I would be the perfect bride for him."

"Oh, Serena, how awful. I mean—Miss Fenton."

"Please do call me Serena. We cannot be formal after our conversation," Serena assured her with a warm smile. "It is such a relief to talk to another female of my difficulties."

"Did you tell Daniel?"

"Yes, and he is the dearest brother. But I could not tell him about Ned's behaviour. I only hinted of Mr. Peabody's disreputable pursuit and he became so angry."

"Daniel? He is such a gentle man," Cleopatra said wonderingly.

"Not when someone or something he loves is threatened. Once, when we were children, the town bully tried to kick our little dog. Daniel thrashed him."

A shiver ran down Cleopatra's spine. Such revelations about her dear Daniel only made her love him all the more.

"What did Mr. Peabody... Did he harm you?"

"No. He wanted only to kiss me. Once, he caught me unawares and his mouth—*faugh!* It was disgusting."

"I have never been kissed," Cleopatra revealed, staring at Serena with something akin to awe.

"I never wish to be kissed again! I shall never marry!" Serena declared in ringing tones.

"Oh."

Catching the disconsolate expression on her new friend's face, Serena asked, "Have I distressed you?"

"Why—no. It is simply that I know Daniel hopes—that is, with you to assist Daniel, he will never—oh, my!" Cleopatra's cheeks grew rosier than ever with her confusion.

Serena stopped the other young lady and pulled her around to face her. "You are in love with Daniel?"

Completely overcome with embarrassment, Cleopatra could only stare at her feet and fight the tears which filled her eyes.

Serena ducked her head to discover those tears and patted her companion on the shoulder. "I did not mean to upset you, Cleopatra. I only hoped it might be so."

"You hoped I might be in love with Daniel?"

"Well, of course. You are charming and I wish Daniel to be happy."

"But you have come to live with him," Cleopatra said, as if Serena had deliberately done so to ensure that Daniel did not marry.

"Only because I could not avoid Mr. Peabody in any other way. But my living with Daniel would not prevent you from marrying him. Unless you would not allow me to live... that is, I am sure you would prefer..."

"Oh, no! I would have no objection to your presence," Cleopatra assured her rapidly. "It is just—I have done everything I can to demonstrate to Daniel how deeply I care. He does not care for me, however."

Serena thought of her brother's red face when he had misspoke himself and wasn't sure she agreed with her.

"I had hoped that his need of assistance in parish duties would cause him to consider marriage. But of course with you to assist him, he will have no need of a wife."

Serena's melodious laughter drew the attention of those passing by. "Dear Cleopatra, surely you do not think I could supplant a well-trained wife? I am famous for my temper and lack of patience. Daniel always has to remonstrate with me." With a smile, she said, "I am sure you are much better suited to assist Daniel."

"I have already done so for two years, but he has never shown me more than friendship."

"And did you receive no proposals while in London?"

"Oh, yes, several, though most were interested in the portion my brother settled upon me when he became the Earl of Granville."

"You truly love Daniel?"

"With all my heart," Cleopatra said simply.

"Then we must discover a way to bring about your marriage," Serena assured her just as they reached the end of the little village.

CHAPTER THREE

CLEOPATRA STIRRED HER TEA as she considered the events of the past two days. Her plan, which had evolved from her discussions with her brother, Daniel, and Serena, was risky and more than a little traitorous. To plot against one's loved ones was not commendable, but she had only until spring to convince Daniel that he could not live without her.

"Are you going to stir that demmed tea for the rest of your life?" Augustus demanded, his face hidden behind his hands.

"Sorry," Cleopatra said. With a look at her brother, she asked, "Did you spend the evening at Ben Tyler's?" The local tavern was a favourite place for young bucks in the area. Since their move to the region two years ago, Augustus had consumed more than his fair share of ale.

Raising his head, Augustus glared at her. "No, my inquisitive little sister, I did not."

"Then you must be ill. Let me feel your forehead," Cleopatra said, rising to tend to him.

"You'll do no such thing! I am fine," he growled.

Cleopatra returned to her chair but she kept her blue eyes on her brother. "You do not appear fine."

"Do not go on so, Patty."

"What is Patty going on about?" Marcus asked as he entered the breakfast room.

Augustus's features grew rigid. "Nothing at all, my lord."

Cleopatra shot a pleading look at her older brother. He took note of her wide-eyed gaze and then said calmly, "It is not necessary to be formal at the breakfast table, Auggie."

Since he then turned his back on his troublesome siblings and began filling his plate at the sideboard, Augustus slumped in his chair.

In an effort to distract Marcus from Augustus's state, and to further her own ends, Cleopatra said, "I went for a drive with Miss Fenton yesterday. She is charming."

Marcus looked over his shoulder to say, "I'm not sure it is wise for you to be seen with such a hoyden."

"Oh, Marcus, she was beautifully behaved. I'm certain the day before was an exception."

"What did she do, fail to grovel when introduced to the Earl of Granville?" Augustus growled.

Marcus's lips tightened, but before he could speak, Cleopatra rushed in. "Auggie! How can you say such a thing? Marcus may be har—I mean, he may insist on certain behaviour, but he never asks anyone to lick his boots!"

"Not a particularly ladylike expression, my dear, but I appreciate the sentiment." Since there was the glimmer of a smile in his bright blue eyes, Cleopatra breathed a sigh of relief.

"I believe I must congratulate Daniel for the salubrious effect his presence has on your temperament, Patty," Marcus added, a definite twinkle in his eye.

With a wide grin, Cleopatra said, "I do not mind, if you can convince him to make it a permanent arrangement. Of course some credit should go to Miss Fenton. I'm learning to deal with my brothers by observing her."

Marcus gave her a sceptical look, but Auggie came out of his trance and stared at his brother. "You would permit the sister of the Earl of Granville to stoop so low as to marry a vicar?"

His snide tones chased away Patty's patience. Before she could protest, however, Marcus's icy words intervened.

"Sir, you forget yourself once too often. If you cannot maintain at least a modicum of civilized behaviour, please excuse yourself."

Pale faced, Augustus toppled his chair as he stood abruptly and strode from the room.

After several moments of silence, Marcus spoke roughly. "What is the matter with that boy? In the past, we dealt with each other fairly well, but lately—"

"I pray you will be patient with him, Marcus. Since you came into the title, all our lives have changed."

With a sigh, Marcus nodded. "I shall try, Patty, but I cannot accept the sort of behaviour he just now demonstrated."

"I know. Perhaps a distraction would ease his... his boredom." She didn't really believe boredom to be the source of Auggie's difficulties, but that theory would serve her well.

"I have no interest in catering to his boorishness."

After looking at her brother's hardened features, his dark brows snapped together over glacial eyes, Cleopatra tried another tack. "Truly, Marcus, as you are the Earl of Granville, your neighbours will expect you to have an entertainment to mark our return from London. And Daniel advised me of his request to you regarding his sister. Why do we not have an entertainment to honour Miss Fenton?"

"Don't you think such consideration might be inappropriate for a—"

"A vicar's sister?" Cleopatra challenged.

"My dear, you defended me from Auggie's accusation. Have you then changed your mind?"

"No, but—"

"I was going to say a young lady not experienced in Society's ways."

"But she is, Marcus. Her behaviour yesterday was totally unexceptionable, I swear to you."

"Patty, riding in a carriage for half an hour is less demanding than being the honoured guest at an evening entertainment. The young woman probably does not have the proper garments for such an appearance, either."

"You have not even given her a chance, Marcus. Come with me to call on Daniel and his sister. You will see how well behaved Miss Fenton is."

Marcus considered her request and finally agreed. "Very well, but we mustn't stay overlong. I have much to do on the estate."

"And we may consider the entertainment?" Cleopatra asked.

"Perhaps. I make no promises."

OVER THE HILL, the vicarage was peaceful, for the vicar was at work in his study preparing a new sermon for the approaching Sabbath. It was pleasurable having his sister in his house. He had missed her, but had thought it would be best for her to remain with Mildred.

There was no future for a young woman who did not marry. Society considered them failures and relegated them to the back parlours, tending their nieces and nephews and being at the beck and call of wealthy relatives. Or even worse, they might spend their lives teaching others' children for a meagre sum sure to keep them poverty-stricken all their days.

Now Serena's future was up to him. She deserved happiness. And in spite of his misgivings about his role as Cupid, he would pursue his goal. With a shake of his head, he pulled his thoughts back to his sermon.

After a brief knock, Serena, looking all merry brightness in her yellow muslin gown and auburn curls, slipped into his study. Without hesitation, she circled the big desk and bent to put her arms about her brother's neck.

He returned the embrace but his gaze searched her features. "Is anything amiss, Serena?"

"Oh, no, Daniel. It is just that I am so grateful to be here. You cannot imagine the relief I feel having removed from Mildred's household. I lived with constant turmoil and harassment. I could do nothing correctly." She shuddered as her thoughts dwelt on the past three years.

"I am so sorry, my dear. I thought you would have the opportunity to—" Daniel broke off to look warily at his sister.

"Well, I did not, and I do not care about marrying. I shall be content to remain with you." Serena moved away from his desk to look at the books on a nearby shelf as she said with studied casualness, "Unless you have matrimonial plans?"

"Me? Why, no, I don't." Many years' experience with sisters made him add, "Why do you ask?"

"You seem so anxious to find an eligible parti for me, I thought I might return the favour." Her gaze met his briefly, a teasing smile on her face, before she turned back to the bookshelf. "Besides, I think Miss Browne is quite attractive and most genteel."

"Of course she is," Daniel replied wryly. "She is also the sister of an earl. And her brother has ambitious plans for his sister, my dear. She will be the wife of someone of higher standing."

"Even if she does not desire it?"

Daniel's features closed and he returned his gaze to his notes. "She will eventually find the right man."

"And I am sure Lord Granville will insist that she do so," Serena said, a tinge of bitterness in her voice.

"Marcus is no monster," Daniel said sharply, looking at his sister again. "It is his duty to provide a husband for Miss Browne."

His bleak expression touched her heart, and Serena resolved to assist her beloved brother, just as he had rescued her from Mildred.

"Ah, well, it is no concern of mine, but I find Miss Browne to be most congenial." When her brother gave no response, Serena turned towards the door. "I believe I shall walk to the village and purchase some embroidery threads."

"Very well, my dear. I shall see you at dinner."

Serena knew he had already turned his thoughts to his work. Such a dear, kind brother. She would ensure his happiness.

AUGUSTUS SAT hunched over the big desk in the study. The half-filled sheet of paper was dotted with ink splotches and scratched-out words. Slowly he read over what he had written.

Dear Tolly,
Sorry. I couldn't keep our rendezvous as my brother had urgent need of me. I'm not exactly sure of the date of my return, but I shall communicate with you as soon as I arrive in Town and we shall settle our agreement.

Auggie

Surely, Tollersham would accept this delay. After all, it wasn't as if he were trying to go back on his word. He wished he could, but a gentleman always kept his word. A bitter laugh escaped him.

"You have found something to amuse you?" Marcus asked as he entered the study.

With a glare, Augustus replied gruffly, "No."

"Patty and I are calling on the vicar and his sister. Would you care to accompany us?"

"Why? Are you hoping to marry me off to someone pious and saintly?" Augustus frowned as he noted a distinct twinkle in his brother's eye.

"Don't look for hidden reasons, Auggie. I simply offered in an attempt to amuse you." Before Augustus could reply, he murmured, "Besides, I would not describe Miss Fenton with such words."

"Perhaps I *will* accompany you. It could not be more dull than remaining here."

Augustus's disgruntled remark drew an unanswerable question from his brother. "And yet you left the excitement of London to join us?"

Ignoring Marcus's question, he prepared his letter for the post. "I'll just give this to Lawrence and then I'll be ready."

"Do not rush. I'm sure Patty will be patient." After Augustus left the room, Marcus crossed over to the desk and straightened out one of the numerous crumpled pieces of paper his brother had left behind. He frowned at the half-completed letter. He had had urgent need of Auggie?

With a sigh, Marcus swept the pieces of paper into the fire burning in the grate. Whatever Augustus had fallen into this time, he would be required to see him through. Their elevation two years ago to wealth and rank had turned Augustus's head. Marcus hoped that soon he would recognize the responsibilities as well as the pleasures of being heir to the Earl of Granville.

Perhaps he should shift some of his duties to Auggie's shoulders since his brother had made himself available. It might be an interesting experience for them both.

As THE BAROUCHE covered the short distance carrying the Earl of Granville's family to the vicarage, Marcus put his new plan to the touch.

"Auggie, I wondered if you would help with some of the estate work since you are here. I have a great deal of paper work to do, and Murchison wishes to show me some fences which need repairing."

"Murchison won't want to deal with me," Augustus growled, not meeting his brother's gaze.

"Murchison will be pleased to deal with the Earl of Granville's heir. If I were to have an accident tomorrow, you would step into my place. Murchison knows that as well as anyone."

Augustus gauged the sincerity in his brother's face. "Very well. I might as well earn my keep."

"Thank you," Marcus replied, a satisfied smile on his face.

Cleopatra had watched the exchange between her brothers with relief. They had been at loggerheads most of the Season. Marcus had complained of Augustus's heavy drinking and gaming and had refused to advance any of his allowance. Augustus had accused his brother of being a clutch purse and forcing him to live below the standards necessary for the heir to an earldom.

In fact, Augustus had been forced to give up his bachelor digs and join his brother and sister in the Granville mansion because of his many debts. Their time together had not been enjoyable, particularly since Marcus was also displeased that his sister refused all matrimonial offers.

Cleopatra sighed. If Marcus and Augustus worked out their difficulties and she brought Daniel up to scratch, perhaps they could be happy once again.

SERENA STROLLED down the lane that led to the vicarage, at peace with the world. Already she was able to forget the contentious years with Mildred.

As she arrived at the vicarage, the forlorn figure of a little boy stood beneath the spreading branches of the large oak tree which sheltered the front of the vicarage.

Bending down, Serena smiled at the boy's drooping lips. "Hello. Is something the matter?"

As he turned towards her, Serena noticed his bandaged arm, wrapped in a grubby sling. "I believe you have already had some difficulty," she said, reaching out a finger to touch his arm.

"It's broken," he muttered.

"Is that why you're upset?"

"Naw. 'Twas broken a while back. I'm sad 'cause I can't climb the tree."

Serena stood up and ruffled the boy's hair. "It won't be long before you are able to climb it. You must be patient."

"But my kitten! I'm afeared he'll get sick in the cold air t'night. Or get lost. He don't know the way home yet."

Serena's gaze followed the direction in which the little boy pointed. Way up among the autumn leaves, she caught a glimpse of movement.

"He's not very big, your cat," she murmured, bending back down.

"No." With a look of wonder in his eyes, the little boy reached up and touched an auburn curl that had escaped Serena's poke bonnet. "That's the same colour as Cinnamon."

It took only a second to realize the child was referring to his kitten and not the spice. With a smile, Serena said, "Well, since we have so much in common, I must assist in saving Cinnamon."

"But what kin you do? Someone must climb the tree, and I kin't. And you're a female!"

"Before I grew up," Serena whispered, as if she were sharing an important secret, "I was a first rate tree climber." With a wink, she handed the little boy her package of embroidery threads and her reticule, removed her bonnet and cloak and placed them beside the tree and swung up to the first branch of the oak with amazing ease.

"WHY ARE WE VISITING the vicar, anyway?" Augustus demanded. "Can't he come to the house if you need to talk to him?"

Marcus lifted one brow. "And have him believe I feel him beneath me, Auggie?"

Since he had accused his brother of such snobbery only that morning, Augustus's cheeks flushed with colour.

"Oh, look, there is Tommy Black. Mrs. Washburn said he broke his arm," Cleopatra added as the barouche drew to a stop before the vicarage. "I wonder why he is staring up at the tree."

Marcus descended from the carriage and turned to assist his sister, waving away the footman. "I'm sure he will tell you if you ask."

Augustus followed his sister. "What do you care about some brat wasting his time looking up a tree?"

"Because he might—hello, Tommy," Cleopatra called as the little boy turned round and saw them.

The three adults were surprised to see a look of fear flash across his freckled face as he turned back to the tree with a sense of urgency.

Marcus frowned. Striding over to the boy, he asked, "Is something wrong?"

The child continued to stare up into the tree. "My kitten is up t'tree."

"Ah. Well, that is a matter of some import. I'll have my footman retrieve it for you." Marcus turned

back to summon his servant, but the child stopped
him.

"But, my lord, *she's* already a gettin' 'im."

Whirling round and staring up, Marcus just had
time to verify Tommy's statement before he drowned
in a sea of petticoats as Serena fell from the tree.
Both tumbled to the ground and the ominous crack
of a bone breaking, a sound Tommy Black knew all
too well, filled the air.

CHAPTER FOUR

PATTY'S SCREAM and the carriage horses' alarm drew both the vicar and his housekeeper out of doors.

Mr. Fenton hurried to the group gathered under the spreading branches of the old oak. "What is amiss?"

The three servants moved back, leaving Patty and Augustus to attend the fallen. The young man looked up in confusion.

"Some demmed female jumped from the tree onto my brother."

"Auggie, I'm sure Serena—" Patty began.

"Serena?" Daniel gasped at his sister who, with Patty's assistance was pulling down her skirts and struggling to a sitting position. A groan emanating from beneath her reminded everyone of Lord Granville.

"Marcus? Are you all right?"

The man did not answer his sister's cry because his teeth were clenched against the pain.

"I heared a bone crack, like mine," Tommy Black muttered, edging closer to the vicar.

With a frown, Mr. Fenton pulled his sister to her feet and urged Patty and Mrs. Washburn to escort her into the vicarage. Lord Granville's white face confirmed the child's diagnosis. Turning to Mr. Browne, the vicar ordered, "Send one of your servants to fetch the doctor."

Shaken by his brother's accident, Augustus meekly followed orders. Mr. Fenton knelt down beside his friend. "Marcus? We have sent for Doctor Capps. Do you think you can move inside? We shall be able to make you more comfortable there."

"I don't think I shall ever be comfortable again," Lord Granville muttered faintly.

"It don't hurt so bad after a while," Tommy offered, staring at Lord Granville's rapidly swelling wrist. The earl only groaned in response.

Mr. Fenton dispatched the child to demand a cushion from Mrs. Washburn. Then he organized the two remaining footmen and Mr. Browne to assist Lord Granville into the vicarage. When Tommy returned with a blue silk cushion clutched in his grubby hands, Mr. Fenton eased Lord Granville's wrist onto it. Mr. Browne tried to assist him, but the sight of the swollen wrist coupled with his brother's groan had him rushing for the bushes were he retched and returned visibly shaken.

In spite of his set jaw, the corners of Lord Granville's lips curved up in acknowledgement of Mr. Fenton's tolerant smile.

"Perhaps . . . perhaps Auggie could hold open the door for us," Marcus suggested.

Hoping to compensate for his humiliating behaviour, Augustus did his brother's bidding.

With Mr. Fenton supporting his wrist upon the pillow, Lord Granville walked into the vicarage assisted by the two footmen, little Tommy Black following in their wake.

The earl was stretched out on the horsehair sofa, his polished boots hanging over the end, before he realized the room also contained the two young ladies. With pain lacing his words, he said, "Ah, the well-behaved Miss Fenton."

Serena, whose remorse had risen as they assisted the earl to the sofa, felt as if she'd been slapped. Stiffening, she said, "My apologies, my lord. If you had not startled me, I would never have lost my grip."

"A proper female would never have been up a tree!" he roared back.

"I suppose I should sit in the parlour all day doing needlepoint?" she demanded, rising to stare down at him.

"That's what normal females do!"

Mr. Fenton, who had gone to the kitchen to prepare a cold cloth, entered the room to discover that war had erupted. "Serena, please remember that Lord Granville is a guest in our house," Daniel murmured, inserting himself between the two combatants, "*and* in great pain."

He calmly went about his ministrations in the complete silence which followed. Finally, Serena muttered, "I am sorry, my lord."

With his eyes closed, Lord Granville replied, "I was at fault, Miss Fenton. My apologies."

Mrs. Washburn's entrance with a hastily prepared tea-tray ended the awkward moment. The two footmen accompanied the housekeeper back to the kitchen. Patty, who had watched the exchange with dismay, busied herself dispensing tea to those left in the parlour.

The arrival of Doctor Capps provided the two young women with the opportunity to escape from the gentlemen's presence.

"I shall surely be out of favour with my brother," Serena said as she closed the door to her brother's study.

"Were you really climbing the tree to retrieve the kitten?" Patty asked, her eyes wide.

"Of course. Why else would I do so?"

"I have never climbed a tree," Patty confessed.

Serena blinked. "It is a childish thing to do, Patty. Your brother is correct. I am sure Daniel will remind me of proper comportment for a lady later."

"But . . . is it fun, to climb a tree?"

A mischievous grin lit up Serena's face. "Yes, it is wonderful to be so far above the ground. Someday when Daniel is not at home, we shall climb one of the trees behind the vicarage so no one will see us.''

''Could we? But if anything happened, Marcus would never forgive me.''

Serena hugged her new friend. ''He will never discover it, Patty. Besides, I think the earl is rather stuffy.''

In spite of frequently agreeing with Serena's judgement of her brother, Patty could not help but defend him. ''Marcus is only newly come into his title, and...and he has a great deal of responsibility.''

''Yes, of course. I must apologize again.'' Though there was no sign of remorse on her face, Serena's words were all that was polite.

ONCE DOCTOR CAPPS had fashioned a splint and wrapped Lord Granville's arm, he prescribed rest for the remainder of the day, and the wearing of a sling to support the injured bone.

As the doctor hurried out the door to his interrupted watch over a birthing, Lord Granville looked up at his host. ''Daniel, I am sorry for my criticism of your sister.''

Daniel's half smile did not reach his eyes. ''Serena is not always properly behaved, Marcus, but she has a good heart. She would never bring harm to anyone intentionally.''

"I am sure you are right. I was upset about the accident. It was such accursed luck! I know I blamed your sister at first. But of course it was simply an unfortunate accident...even though she had no business climbing trees." He grimaced as a shaft of pain shot through his arm as he carelessly moved it. "It is just that I have so many tasks waiting for me after our long absence in London. I don't know how I shall be able to accomplish anything."

Augustus cleared his throat. "I promised to assist you, Marcus. I will do what I can."

"I appreciate your offer, Auggie, and I had already planned for you to see to a great deal of the outside work, supervising the winter planting and the repairs. But there is enough paperwork to keep me busy all winter without ever setting a foot out of doors."

"Perhaps you could engage a secretary," Daniel suggested. "I would offer to assist you, but there is not enough time as it is to tend to all those in need and prepare my sermons."

"Of course, I would not ask it of you, Daniel. Perhaps Patty will assist me until a secretary can be located."

Daniel thought of the many tasks Patty willingly assumed for him and almost groaned aloud. With a sigh, he offered Lord Granville another cup of tea before he set out on the tiring transfer to the big house on the hill.

"BUT MARCUS, I cannot," Patty protested. The hurt swiftly hidden in her brother's eyes drew an explanation from her. "It is not that I am unwilling to assist you. But I have already volunteered to help Daniel with many of his projects. I would not have time to do both."

Augustus, standing beside his brother's bed, expressed surprise. "I should think your brother's needs would come before those of Mr. Fenton."

Her cheeks red, Patty sent a silent plea to her elder brother.

With a rueful grin, Lord Granville came to her rescue. "Patty and I have an, er, special agreement... that is, an understanding, Auggie. I fully comprehend her response." He avoided his brother's gaze.

"Well, I do not, and I think—"

"I know!" Patty interrupted. "Oh, Marcus, the perfect plan. Serena shall be your secretary!"

Both brothers stared at her as if she'd lost her wits. Finally, Marcus responded, "Thank you, Patty, but I believe I shall find another solution."

"I should think so," Auggie agreed. "Silliest idea I've ever heard. Can't have a tree-climbing hoyden turned loose among Marcus's papers. She'd destroy everything!"

"She would not! Serena would be perfect."

"You don't know that!" Auggie retorted.

"Yes, I do. Besides, she only climbed the tree to assist little Tommy. She has a kind heart." She paused to turn determined eyes on her elder brother. "And Marcus, you haven't forgotten our agreement, have you?"

The wary look in her brother's eyes brought a smile to Patty's lips. "I can see you have not. And I believe engaging Serena to assist you may make it possible for me to win."

"Win? You have a wager?" Auggie stared at the other two.

"Not precisely," Patty said, her gaze on her elder brother.

"Patty," Marcus protested, "surely you do not consider this incident to fall into the territory of our agreement?"

"But I do, Marcus. I shall help Daniel as planned, and Serena will assist you—only until you are able to locate a real secretary."

"We do not even know that Miss Fenton is capable of working as my secretary," Marcus said, searching for an escape.

"I shall return to the vicarage at once to discover whether she is, and if she will agree to assist us." Without waiting for a protest from either brother, Patty whisked out of the room.

Marcus stared at the door, dismay writ on his face.

"What agreement is Patty speaking of?"

Shaken from his unpleasant thoughts, Marcus shrugged. "Patty has a maggot in her head about Daniel. She refused all the proposals she received because she hopes to become Mrs. Fenton. I have allowed her until the beginning of the next Season to bring him up to scratch. If she is not successful, then she must accept one of her other suitors."

Augustus frowned. "Patty should not be forced into an unpleasant marriage."

"I do not wish her to be unhappy, Augustus, but an unmarried woman has no place in Society. It is my duty to ensure Patty's future."

"I do not understand why you must accept Miss Fenton as your secretary, even so. That has nothing to say to Patty's plan, does it?"

Marcus subsided against the pillows. "I wish that were true. But in my desire to assist her, I agreed to any reasonable request that would bring her into Daniel's company. Since she would have to give up working with him to act as my secretary, I'm afraid it has a great deal to say to Patty's plan."

PATTY SILENTLY URGED the horses to go faster even as she sat sedately in her brother's carriage. Marcus's accident would further *both* Patty's plans: Serena would be closeted with Marcus for long periods, and Patty would have Daniel to herself.

When the carriage stopped in front of the vicarage, Patty hopped down before the footman could assist her, eager to speak with Daniel.

Escorted into his study, Patty firmly closed the door before turning to face the Vicar.

"Patty, your brother said you should not—"

"Oh, pooh! Marcus did not mean it. Besides, what I have to say is—is a secret."

Daniel's eyebrows rose as he escorted the petite young lady to the sofa. "A secret? You are not planning anything improper, are you, Patty? Because I could not support you in that event."

"Of course not, Daniel. I have Marcus's approval for what I am about to suggest. Well, most of it, anyway." She leaned forward, her cheeks rosy and her light blue eyes sparkling, and Daniel almost forgot her words. "I have devised a wonderful scheme to further your plans."

"My plans?"

"For Serena and Marcus," Patty reminded him anxiously.

"Oh! Of course, but—I am not sure. After today—"

"The events of today have provided the answer. Marcus has a great deal of paperwork to do, and he can no longer see to it himself because of his broken wrist. Serena shall act as his secretary!"

"Serena?"

"She can read and write, can she not?"

"Of course she can. She shared my tutors and I have since given her additional studies. She is well educated."

"Splendid. Then Marcus will accept her services as secretary until an appropriate replacement can be found." When there was no response from the vicar, Patty added impatiently, "Don't you see, Daniel? They will be constantly together, and Serena can show Marcus how prettily behaved she is. And she is so beautiful that Marcus cannot help but fall in love with her."

She was disappointed by Daniel's response. Though he considered her words, his brows furrowed in thought, Patty had hoped for instant endorsement of her clever plan.

She deemed it time to force his hand. "If Serena does not serve as Marcus's secretary, I must volunteer, and I shall not be able to assist you as we had both planned."

Sadness fell on Daniel's features. "I would not want to keep you from your sisterly duties."

"Daniel Fenton! If you do not want my assistance, you should say so."

The tears shining in her eyes compelled him to honesty. "You know it is not that, Patty." He reached a hand out to clasp hers. "Your presence adds too much to my ministry, to those I serve. I do not wish to forfeit your assistance. But I must also accept that the day may come when you leave to live your own life.''

With a decided sniff, Patty drew his hand to rest against her cheek. ''That day will not arrive, Daniel.'' Her eyes pleaded with him to understand, but he gently slid his hand from hers and stood, finding her too disturbing at such close quarters.

''I cannot resist the temptation to accept your services. I admit I still have hopes for Marcus and Serena, and your plan will serve my purposes admirably.'' He turned to face her once more. ''You are sure Marcus has no objection to Serena? He appeared today to have some further doubts about her behaviour.''

''Only as a result of his pain, Daniel. He admitted later that it was an accident. And he agreed to my plan...even if he has no knowledge of the true reason behind it. Will you speak to Serena?''

Daniel stood in thought before smiling at Patty. ''I think we must approach her together. She seems no more receptive to your brother than he is to her.''

Patty rose and linked her arm through Daniel's. ''I shall gladly assist you, Daniel. We can always suggest it would seem only fair since her accident caused Marcus to break his wrist.''

''Very well. Let us join Serena for tea in the parlour and put the proposition to her.''

Serena was awaiting her brother's presence for tea, and she expressed pleasure that Patty was joining

them. As much as she loved her brother, his brief
lecture on deportment had rather put her back up.
She did not consider herself to have been in the
wrong. After all, she had only wished to help the
boy. Perhaps Patty would be an agreeable distraction for brother and sister just now.

After the cups had been filled and passed round,
Serena very properly asked after the earl's recovery,
willing to go that far to appease her brother. Patty
seized the opportunity to present her plan.

"He is recovering nicely now that the pain has
subsided. However, he is most concerned about the
work piling up, awaiting his attention."

Serena made a suitable rejoinder, though her irritation with the earl allowed little interest in his difficulties.

"I am concerned that he will fall into the dismals
and wondered if you might assist him."

Serena's green eyes snapped to attention as she fo-
cused on her new friend. "I beg your pardon? I do
not understand."

A sideways look from Patty brought Daniel into
the conversation. "Patty suggested you might act as
Marcus's secretary for a short time, until he locates
a suitable person for the position. It would ease his
mind considerably."

Serena stared at first her brother and then the
young lady beside him. Finally, her gaze returned to
Daniel. "Me? Did you not hear the man today? He

considers me to be quite poorly behaved. And he is not the only one," she muttered, her eyes flashing at her brother.

"Serena, my love, I did not mean—I only wished you to consider your actions. You know I only have your best interests at heart."

"Besides, it is the brotherly thing to do, to scold one's sister. Marcus is forever doing so," Patty added with a cheerful smile.

"But I know nothing about such work, and I daresay Lord Granville would not tolerate me in the position."

"Nonsense," Daniel asserted. "You are well educated, probably more so than most men. You write a neat hand and your sums were always more accurate than mine. You always handled the budget for Mama, paying the bills and managing the house."

"Yes, and I enjoyed doing so. But Mama was not the Earl of Granville," Serena said, her back ramrod straight.

"Marcus is in desperate need," Patty said softly. "He is agreeable to your taking on the position. I have already obtained his assent."

Serena's brows rose. "What did you have to relinquish in return?"

As Daniel protested his sister's words, Patty laughed. "Nothing, I assure you, that I had not already promised. Oh, Serena, you sounded just like Marcus. I know the two of you will deal famously."

"We shall do no such thing," Serena said firmly. "I am sorry that your brother was injured, but it was an accident. After three years of Mildred's disapproval, I have no desire to allow the earl to step in and do the same."

"Serena—" Daniel began before Mrs. Washburn interrupted him.

"Sir, that Roddy McGuire's at the back door askin' to speak with you, personal."

Daniel hesitated, torn between appealing to his sister and his clerical duties. Duty won and he rose to follow Mrs. Washburn. "I shall return in a moment," he warned his sister as he hurried from the room.

Before Serena could introduce another subject, Patty rushed into speech. "Please, Serena, you must agree to assist my brother. Otherwise, I shall have to do so. And then I could not assist Daniel." Even as Serena opened her lips to protest again, Patty looked at her forlornly to add, "How shall I convince Daniel to marry me, otherwise? And you said you had no objection to me."

"Of course I do not, Patty, but—"

"Please, Serena?"

Serena did not understand how her brother had resisted Miss Cleopatra Browne even once if she looked at him with those china-blue eyes. With a shrug, she conceded defeat. "Very well, Patty, but I cannot promise your brother will be pleased. I will not tolerate his condescending attitude."

"Of course not," Patty agreed, but Serena felt Patty was more pleased with her success than interested in Serena's difficulties with her brother.

Daniel entered at that moment, determination written across his face. "Now, Serena—" he began again.

"Your sister has graciously agreed to assist my brother," Patty broke in with a bemusing smile.

Daniel stopped abruptly to stare first at Serena then at Patty. "How...how good of her," he muttered while he wondered what could have altered his stubborn sister's mind.

"Yes, isn't it?" Patty turned back to Serena. "I think we should allow Marcus a day's rest, so if you could come to the house in two days' time, I'm sure he will be delighted to accept your services."

"Delighted?" Serena questioned, her gaze disbelieving.

"Delighted," Patty restated firmly. "Otherwise, he will be reduced to employing Augustus, and *he* cannot spell at all."

CHAPTER FIVE

TWO DAYS LATER, Mr. Fenton and his sister strolled up the hill to the imposing house which dominated the neighbourhood. Few words were spoken as each thought about coming events.

As they approached the front steps, however, Serena's hand slipped beneath her brother's arm, reminding him of her presence. He looked down at her with a smile as he patted her hand. "You must not be at odds with your new employer, Serena. Marcus—Lord Granville—is a good man, but he will expect your obedience."

"A fine gentleman with a fine temper," Serena muttered.

Daniel laughed. "Patty is correct. You and Marcus are a good deal alike. You must admit that for you to complain of someone else's temper is akin to the pot calling the kettle black, my dear."

"I only occasionally become overheated, Daniel," Serena protested, her lips pressed into a prim line.

"And you are never mischievous, either," Daniel said solemnly.

Serena's honesty was tried too severely by her brother's teasing. With a peal of laughter, her eyes dancing, she shook her head. "Of course not, Daniel. It has always been my brother who led me astray."

"Shame on you, Serena, for saying such things about a man of the cloth."

Serena was smiling up at her brother when the austere Lawrence opened the door.

She sobered at once, but her brother remained at ease. "Good morning, Lawrence. Is Lord Granville at home?"

The stately butler unbent enough to give what Serena suspected was a smile, though it was so brief that she could not be sure.

"Of course, Mr. Fenton. If you will wait, I shall announce you."

As the butler left them, Serena stared at the gracious entry hall, its black and white tiles gleaming and the furniture polished to a brilliant shine. Further along, a fire crackled merrily in a huge fireplace, casting reflections on the Oriental vases gracing the mantelpiece.

"How beautiful," Serena murmured, unconsciously pulled further into the room. "Daniel, is this not the most beautiful hall you have ever seen?" she demanded.

Lord Granville, emerging from the breakfast room to hear her last comment, softened towards the young lady who had disturbed his every waking thought since they had met.

"I am glad you are pleased," he said smoothly before turning to greet Daniel. "We are lingering over our tea. Won't you both join us for a second cup?"

Serena, not happy to have been caught gawking, left it to Daniel to respond.

"I would not be averse to a cup, if it is no bother," he replied. "Serena?"

"Oh, yes, that will be lovely." She looked coolly at Lord Granville, wanting him to know she was not overly impressed with either his home or his hospitality. Daniel took her arm when Marcus gestured for them to precede him.

Patty was still at the table and greeted both of them happily. She would have liked to suggest that Daniel and Serena take their breakfast with them each morning, but she feared Daniel would think her forward. She poured them both cups of tea and then refilled her brother's cup, adding the sugar and cream he took.

"Here, Marcus, I have prepared it just as you like it. Serena, when tea is served in the afternoon, you must add one spoon of sugar and just a little cream."

"Patty, I am capable of preparing my own tea," Marcus protested.

"Of course you are, Marcus, but with your injured wrist, it is more difficult for you."

"I have no objection to preparing your tea, my lord." Serena lifted her own cup to avoid looking at the irritated gentleman seated at the head of the table, though she secretly enjoyed his discomfiture.

"Thank you, Miss Fenton, but I require a secretary, not a nursery maid."

He could drown in his own teacup before she'd lift a finger to assist him, Serena vowed, but she said nothing aloud. After all, she had promised her brother to be on her best behaviour.

"Daniel, what are your plans for this morning?" Patty asked, abandoning the other two for a more reasonable guest.

"I must visit Mrs. Tenpenny. I have heard she is not well."

"Oh, may I accompany you? I'll instruct Cook to prepare a basket which we shall take to her. Did you walk? I'm sure Marcus will be glad to lend us his carriage. Let me advise Lawrence as to our needs and fetch my cloak." Like a whirlwind, Patty quit the room before anyone could say a word.

"If you are not careful, Daniel, my little sister will order your life to her liking," Marcus observed.

"Miss Browne's enthusiasm is a great encouragement to me." Daniel studied his hands, folded before him on the table.

Lord Granville, frustration apparent in his face, rose and gestured for the vicar to follow him. In the entry hall, he said, "Daniel, my comments of the other day were not directed to you, and well you know it.''

"Everything you said was true.''

"I was trying to protect *you* as much as Patty,'' Marcus insisted, his voice rising.

Daniel said nothing.

Marcus studied his friend, recognizing his implacable expression. Early on, he had discovered Daniel would not be turned from something he believed was right. As good and kind as he was, he had the determination of a bullock. Shaking his head, Marcus felt a moment of pity for his sister.

Patty came down the stairway, her cheeks flushed and her eyes sparkling, looking not in the least need of pity. "I am ready, Daniel.''

"Very well, Miss Browne. Is your maid ready to accompany us?''

A look of incredulity flickered across Patty's face as she glanced first at Daniel and then at Marcus. "No, of course not. What has occurred?''

Neither man had an answer for her question and she asked, "Did you have a disagreement?''

"You are suggesting nonsense, Miss Browne,'' Daniel said, his tone brisk. "Shall we go? Mrs. Tenpenny has need of us.''

Though she shot a frown at her brother, Patty could never resist Daniel. She took his proffered arm and accompanied him out of the house.

Lord Granville, far from pleased, returned to the dining room to collect his new secretary. "If you are ready, Miss Fenton, we shall withdraw to the study."

Serena stood and repeated the apology her brother insisted was Lord Granville's due. "My lord, I apologize again for being the cause of your distress."

His mind still on the problem of his sister and the vicar, Marcus muttered, "It was an accident, Miss Fenton, nothing more. Shall we go? We have a great deal of work awaiting us."

He escorted her to the study. In spite of her irritation with the man for so cavalierly dismissing her apology, Serena was amazed at the beauty of her surroundings. She wandered among the bookshelves, her fingers trailing over the leather bindings, pausing occasionally as she discovered a volume she particularly loved.

Marcus watched her in surprise. The rapture which played across her features was enlightening. She was a woman with a passion for books, devoted to her brother. What else did she care passionately about? he wondered. And how would it feel to be the object of that passion, wrapped as it was in her beauty? He shook himself and recalled Serena to their purpose in gruff tones in order to mask his discomfort.

Serena quickly took up a position near the tall, powerful man's desk, close enough to observe the papers he wished to show her. After all, she had not expected congeniality from him—and it was a good thing, she thought wryly, for none would be forth-coming.

SEVERAL HOURS LATER, Marcus sat back in his chair, rubbing the forefinger of his left hand over his lips as he studied the bent head at a table across the room. Miss Fenton, for all her passion, her uncontrolled impulses, was proving herself a more than adequate secretary. Nonsense, he reprimanded himself: she was a superb assistant. Her understanding was far superior to that of many of the noblemen he had encountered in the House of Lords.

Her penmanship was more legible than his own when his arm was not broken. Moreover, her capacity for work far outweighed Augustus's and was equal to his own, he realized. Perhaps breaking a bone was not such a catastrophe, after all.

Serena looked up to find his lordship's eyes upon her. "Is there something more, my lord?"

"No, Miss Fenton. I was just considering my next project."

"I shall be finished with this letter shortly."

"Fine, fine."

She returned to her work, but she felt his gaze remain on her. In truth, the past two hours had been enjoyable, as long as she forgot for whom she worked. But with his attention focussed upon her, she found her chores more difficult.

"Your brother is a stubborn man."

Serena turned, laying the pen carefully beside the paper on which she was working. "My brother is a wonderful man." Her firmness left no room for disagreement.

"Of course. But is no less stubborn for all that."

Serena's smile peeped out. "True."

Surprisingly to both of them, Marcus returned her smile. "I believe I offended him the other day, and he will not accept my apology."

"How did you offend him?"

"I interrupted one of their private interviews to remonstrate with Patty about her lack of propriety. It seems your brother assumed the setdown was meant for him. That is why he addressed Patty as Miss Browne in my presence this morning. I expect a rare trimming from her when she returns."

Serena laced her fingers together in her lap. "Daniel considers you to be his friend. I'm sure he is not angry with you. He assured me just this morning that you are a good man."

Standing, Marcus walked over to the fireplace and leaned against the mantel. "Daniel is generous. My goodness, as he terms it, has been greatly supported and encouraged by him. I know no man as good as Daniel."

He was rewarded for his words by a brilliant smile from Miss Fenton.

"My lord, my estimation of you has risen considerably. I can see you are a man of great good sense."

A wry grin crossed his face. "And I count Daniel a lucky man to have two such young ladies in admiration of him."

"Two? Oh, you mean Patty—I mean, Miss Browne."

"Can you doubt it? She fairly radiates happiness when in Daniel's presence."

Serena studied him carefully. She read no condemnation in his expression, but she wished to be sure. "You ... you have no reservations about Patty's feelings for Daniel?"

"Lord, no! I should be delighted if he would take her off my hands!" At Serena's frown, he raised a hand in protest. "I love my sister, Miss Fenton, but the child is driving me insane in her quest for Daniel."

"But if you have no objection, why has he not—I mean, I believe my brother cares for Patty, as well. I thought—" She broke off in confusion, her cheeks red.

"Ah, that I was the villain? No, no, it is not me. While I know Daniel admires Patty, friendship does not equate to love. It could very well be that Patty's feelings are not returned."

Though his smile remained, Serena caught the concern in the man's words. "I have reason to believe that is not the case, my lord, and I believe Daniel and Patty would make a wonderful couple. I have vowed to assist Patty in her quest, but Daniel avoids the subject whenever I broach it.''

"You are assisting Patty just by being here. Otherwise, she would have to give up her time with Daniel to assist me.''

Serena arched her brows. "My very reason for agreeing to the task, my lord. Also, I fear I would be a dreadful assistant for Daniel. Even my knitting is disastrous.''

"Have you no interest in domestic subjects?''

"I am an able housekeeper,'' Serena assured him, not wishing to appear completely devoid of feminine accomplishments before this man. "I maintained my mother's house for three years before her death.''

"You must have done so at a very early age,'' Marcus observed, regarding her youthful beauty.

"I was thirteen when I first began. Mildred, our sister, was eighteen and newly married when Mama became ill. Daniel was just out of school and in his first position near London. There was no one else but myself to manage the household.''

"Could not you and your mother have lived with your married sister?''

"No,'' Serena said simply. With a shudder, she added, "Three years living with Mildred after Mama's death was more than enough.'' Her gaze swung to the man looking down at her with a pitying expression and she gasped. "I beg your pardon, my lord. I am wasting your time with my gossip. I shall finish this letter at once.''

Marcus returned to his desk, but his thoughts remained with his new secretary. She was beautiful and intelligent—a rare combination, he had discovered the past two years in London. Daniel was right to seek a good marriage for her. He supposed he must do what he could to assist him, though he could think of no one in the neighbourhood with the strength to control her irrepressible spirit. His own visage floated before his eyes but was quickly dismissed. The Earl of Granville's wife must be above reproach.

ONCE THEY WERE SEATED in Marcus's barouche, Patty demanded an explanation from Daniel to account for his sudden change of behaviour.

''What are you talking about, my dear?'' His bland smile did not deter her, however.

''You know exactly what I refer to. Did Marcus offend you in any way?''

''Of course not.''

''Then why did you address me as Miss Browne and enquire about my maid? I have never requested that Tilly accompany us when we are tending the needy about the parish.''

''That is to my discredit. I did not consider your reputation before. Now that Marcus has brought it to my attention, we must take more care. On future trips I prefer that you have Tilly accompany us.''

''I shall do no such thing!'' Patty protested. She leaned towards the love of her life, her heart breaking. ''Daniel, do you not understand? I do not care what anyone should think. I want only to work at your side.''

Daniel looked down at her rosy cheeks, her full lips, her beautiful eyes and swallowed the lump in his throat. Why God chose to offer him such temptation he did not know, but he only hoped he would not be required to play the role of Job, with Patty as his temptress.

He doubted that he possessed the strength to hold his heart in check for another year. He had promised himself he would not approach Marcus again until after Patty had had three Seasons to select a husband. If none of the titles or fortunes appealed to her after that time, perhaps then Marcus would consider him as a suitor.

''Patty, you must know I am not indifferent to you. But you must also allow that the situation is quite unsuitable. You should fulfill your proper role in Society.''

Daniel stared straight ahead and therefore missed the determined light in the eyes of the diminutive lady seated next to him. ''That is my intention, kind sir,'' she muttered, and ignored the surprise on his face.

SERENA WAS STARTLED when the study door opened and Lawrence stepped into the room. "Luncheon is served, my lord."

She looked over at the large desk and observed that her employer appeared weary.

"Miss Fenton, Lawrence will show you to a chamber where you may refresh yourself. I shall not join you at table today, if you will excuse me."

At her look of surprise, he muttered, rather than offend her, "I am unable to maintain decent manners as yet with my left hand."

"Please, my lord, do not concern yourself. You must have proper nourishment, and I shall promise not to laugh if you should drop your eating utensil." There was a challenge in both her gaze and her words that made Marcus respond with an abrupt nod. She stood and dipped a brief curtsy before following Lawrence from the room.

In the hallway, she whispered, "Lawrence, could someone prepare a drink with a drop of laudanum for the master? I believe he is in some pain due to his injury."

For the first time, the butler appeared human, smiling slightly. "Yes, Miss Fenton. I shall do so. However, I cannot guarantee the master will take it. He has refused any medicine more than once."

"I shall try to convince him."

When she entered the dining room a few minutes later, Serena discovered Lord Granville's brother in attendance also. Greetings were exchanged and they each took their places.

As Lawrence served the first course, a particularly tasty potato soup, Mr. Browne launched into a detailed account of his inspection of fences that morning. Serena was surprised at his enthusiasm and did not offer a more diverting topic. Perhaps fences would distract Lord Granville.

However, as Mr. Browne's discourse continued through several more servings and Lord Granville appeared to be in considerable pain, Serena decided to exceed her authority. Waiting until the young man ceased speaking to take a bite of the rabbit on his plate, she hurriedly asked, "My lord, did Lawrence bring you any medicine? I particularly asked him to prepare some for you."

Marcus, his head pounding, turned to stare at the young lady on his right. "Yes, he did, Miss Fenton, but I refused it."

He turned back to his brother, but Serena was not so easily defeated. "Lawrence," she called, as the servant was leaving the room, "would you please bring the medicine back?"

Lawrence looked first at his master and then at the young lady. Though he said nothing, he gave a discreet nod to Serena before exiting the room.

"Might I remind you that the man is in my employ, not yours, Miss Fenton?" Marcus growled. Though his temples were throbbing to the point that he could not think straight, Lord Granville did not intend to be ordered about by any young lady.

Serena said nothing to the angry man beside her. Instead, she sought an ally. "Mr. Browne, I believe it would be wise if your brother rested for an hour or two this afternoon after he takes some medicine."

Augustus looked in surprise at the young lady. He had been so taken up with recounting his morning's activities that he had paid scarce attention to the vicar's sister. Now, induced to take a close look at his brother, he noticed for the first time the deep furrow in his forehead.

"You are in pain, Marcus?"

"Nothing of importance, Auggie, just a slight headache."

"My lord, if you will take the medicine and rest for only a little while, I am sure it will go away." Serena's soft voice was soothing in itself, but her words were not.

"I will not be ordered to take to my bed by you, Miss Fenton. As I stated earlier, I require a secretary, not a nursery maid." His anger rose as the pain in his head increased.

What little liking Serena had for the man was fast disappearing in the face of his stubbornness. "And I shall not be held responsible for your distress when you prolong it with your childish obstinacy," she murmured just as Lawrence entered the room with a glass on a silver tray.

Augustus watched the pair in fascination. He had seen women fawn over his brother during the Season, yet this woman seemed bent on angering him. Another look at his brother, however, convinced him she was quite right.

"Come on, old man, take your medicine," he urged, drawing a quelling glance from his brother.

Serena wisely said nothing, pretending a great interest in her meal, though she managed to direct a smile of approval at Mr. Browne.

Lord Granville glared at the young lady and his brother before he turned to the butler. Even the unperturbed Lawrence drew an angry look, but as all three remained silent, he grabbed the glass and downed the cloudy liquid. "There. Now may we find a conversational subject more interesting than my health or lack of it?"

Obliging him by asking a question about the estate, Serena pretended an interest in Augustus's self-important explanation, encouraging the young man to continue talking to her, leaving his brother in peace.

When the meal ended, she informed Lord Granville that the work he had assigned her would occupy her for several hours if he wished to attend to other matters. He eyed her sternly.

"I have no intention of resting, Miss Fenton. I am not a schoolboy to be sent to his bed in the middle of the day."

"Dash it, Marcus, the doctor said you were to rest each day. Miss Fenton has the right of it." Augustus was as surprised as his brother to discover himself supporting the young lady.

Serena was unable to hide her satisfaction as she rose to leave the table. Feeling surrounded by traitors, Lord Granville stood up abruptly. "Very well. If I am to be in your way in the study, Miss Fenton, I shall find other things to occupy my time." Without another word, he stalked from the room.

"I hope I have not offended your brother," Serena said calmly, no regret visible in her expression.

"Don't matter," Auggie assured her. "We do so regularly. He's been difficult to live with since he became an earl. But I must say, Miss Fenton, you put him to rout better than anyone."

Unsure of her response to such praise, Serena returned to the study.

CHAPTER SIX

AFTER THEIR VISIT with Mrs. Tenpenny, Daniel escorted Patty to the carriage but did not enter it himself.

"Thank you for accompanying me, Miss Browne," he said, his gaze flickering over the driver and the footman before returning to Patty's startled face.

"You are not returning with me?" she asked.

"No, I have several others to visit." Without another word, he waved the driver on, stepping away from the carriage.

Patty stared over her shoulder at his diminishing figure. She was strongly reminded of their friendship, which was also diminishing. Her hopes of marriage grew dimmer with each passing day. Marcus was partially at fault; his strictures to her in the presence of Daniel had resulted in his stiff and correct behaviour. Patty longed for a return to the time when she and Daniel had become fast friends, sharing their thoughts. Those moments had sustained her during the long London Seasons, but now she discovered they were as insubstantial as Gunther's famous ices, melting away all too quickly.

Patty pulled herself from her dismals in time to halt the carriage near Mr. Lavender's store. Tomorrow, she would resume the knitting classes, and she required new supplies. She used part of her allowance to purchase wool and needles for the ladies who attended her class. Squaring her shoulders, Patty vowed she would not abandon the ladies just because the vicar had abandoned *her*.

DANIEL STRODE ALONG the path leading to the vicarage, his mind working at an even faster pace. He would have to maintain the distance between himself and Patty for a while longer. It was a matter of honour. He owed friendship and loyalty to Marcus, and he had promised himself he'd wait three years. But Patty was proving too tempting in her sweetness. He was finding the wait nigh impossible.

Not for the first time, Daniel contemplated the prospect of life with Patty as his wife. He could imagine nothing more wonderful. He had felt certain not so long ago that they would marry. Of late, however, some of Marcus's words caused him to wonder if the earl would ever accept him as Patty's husband. And, of course, there was always the possibility Patty would accept another offer for she was becoming impatient with him. Even so, Daniel knew that he could not explain why he did not speak.

With a sigh, he trudged on. He had to place his trust in the Almighty. After all, he was God's servant, and He would provide the proper helpmeet. Daniel only hoped it would be Patty.

"Oh, Mr. Fenton, you have returned," Mrs. Washburn said in greeting. "Shall I bring a tea-tray or are you ready for your luncheon?"

"Luncheon will be fine, Mrs. Washburn. The walk has made me sharp-set."

He was soon seated at table and the housekeeper carried in a tray. An envelope rested on one corner of it. "What's this?"

"Ooh, it's a letter, come this morning. I was going to put it on your desk."

"That's all right. Since I'm dining alone, I'll read it now." He broke the seal and pulled out the letter. With pleasure, he discovered it was from an old school friend, Sir Charles Burroughs, who had served on the Continent with Marcus.

"Old Charlie," he muttered to himself. His amusement quickly turned to concern as he read of the injury his friend had sustained while on the Continent. Though Sir Charles had a large estate in Northumberland, he asked if he might visit with Daniel during his recuperation instead of travelling so far north, a journey which was arduous at the best of times.

While Daniel would always welcome a friend, he decided it might be best to apply to Marcus to offer his comrade-in-arms a guest-room in his house. It occurred to Daniel that competition might make Marcus more aware of Serena's beauty. If he asked Marcus to invite Charlie to stay in the big house, it would thrust him into any flirtation Charlie might set up with Serena.

Though it was not Daniel's desire, Charlie might even qualify as a husband for Serena, should Marcus show no interest. Charlie was a good man, though a trifle high-spirited. A sudden thought troubled him. *What if Patty were attracted to the man?* He gathered his faith to him and hurried to the big house to consult his friend before he changed his mind.

SERENA WORKED STEADILY in the study the remainder of the afternoon without any sign of Lord Granville. She wondered if he had decided to rest, after all, but she refused to ask Lawrence. After she prepared the letters the earl requested, she set to organizing the papers scattered about the desk. How the man found anything was beyond her.

The study door opened and Patty peered around it. "Are you alone?"

"Yes, I am. Your brother has not returned since luncheon."

"Was he difficult to work for?"

"Not at all. He was ever the gentleman," Serena said, silently reflecting that at least it had been true until she ordered the medicine for him. But she kept that thought to herself.

"Come take tea with me, then. I am deep in the dismals and would appreciate a cheerful face." Patty did indeed appear less than her optimistic self.

"Very well. I have completed all the paper work your brother gave me." Serena followed the smaller young lady from the room, wondering what could have overset Patty.

She sat quietly while Lawrence directed his minions in the serving of tea, watching her friend from beneath lowered lashes. Though Patty appeared composed, there was a paleness about her that confirmed something was amiss.

As soon as the servants withdrew, Serena leaned forward. "Patty, what has occurred to overset you?"

"Nothing, really. I fear I am just being silly."

"May we join you?" Marcus asked from the doorway, Augustus behind him.

Serena started. "I have completed all the tasks you gave me, my lord. If there is anything—"

"I have no complaints, Miss Fenton," Marcus said, strolling into the room. "You have earned your tea."

"You must ask Lawrence for more cups, Auggie," Patty said quietly.

"Are you feeling quite the thing?" Marcus demanded, staring at Patty while Augustus retreated to locate the butler.

Her gaze flew to her brother before she looked away. She replied calmly, "Yes, of course. How are *you* feeling? When I returned, Lawrence said you were resting in your room."

Serena kept her gaze fastened on the teacup she held in her hand but she could feel the earl's eyes on her heated cheeks.

"I did not sleep well last night, so I spent the afternoon in quiet contemplation."

"That is most sensible of you, Marcus." Augustus returned, followed by Lawrence with an additional tray, and Patty busied herself pouring for everyone.

"How was your visit with Mrs. Tenpenny?" Marcus asked. Serena noted that he was watching his sister closely while he awaited her answer. He, too, realized Patty was not herself.

"Fine. I left her some of Cook's broth. Perhaps it will make her feel more the thing."

"Should've taken her a bottle of bourbon. Would've made her feel better," Augustus suggested with a laugh.

"The vicar included a bottle of wine in the basket of provisions he brought," Patty assured her brother, ignoring his laughter.

"Maybe this vicar is a right'un, after all."

Before Patty could shush her brother, Lord Granville said stiffly, "You have forgotten that Miss Fenton is this vicar's sister, Augustus. I believe you owe her an apology.''

''Why? I didn't say anything bad about the man. Instead, I praised him.'' Augustus's belligerent words were about to draw him another lecture when Serena intervened.

''You are quite right, sir. Your words were praise indeed. And I might assure you they are well deserved. My brother is a prince among men.'' The charming smile she offered Mr. Browne seemed to have no effect on him, but Lord Granville resented it, even so.

Lawrence entered the room again. ''Mr. Fenton has called, my lord.''

''Show him in, of course, Lawrence, and fetch another cup.''

Lord Granville rose to greet his friend and invited him to join them.

''I thought I might escort Serena home, if you have finished for the day,'' Daniel explained with a smile. However, both Lord Granville and Serena noted that he carefully avoided looking at Patty.

''Of course, but you need not have troubled yourself. I would have called out the carriage. In fact, I can still do so and you can ride as well.''

''Nonsense. Exercise is good for the body.'' Daniel sat down and received a cup of tea from Patty, neither meeting the other's eye. ''In actual fact, I had another reason for calling. Would you have a few minutes to spare me for some private conversation, Marcus?''

Lord Granville wondered if the topic for discussion would be his sister. Something was certainly in the wind. "Of course, Daniel. Shall we repair to the study?''

Before the others said anything, the two men had left the salon. Both Augustus and Serena looked to Patty.

"I do not know what Dan—Mr. Fenton—wishes to discuss,'' she assured the other two hastily. "He said nothing to me of special interest.''

Serena was forced to control her curiosity, while Augustus seemed oblivious to the many currents swirling about him. He spent the rest of tea discussing his brother's excellent stables.

DANIEL PULLED the letter from his pocket before taking a seat. "This was delivered today. I thought you might care to read it.''

Lord Granville took the letter, realizing his hope that Daniel had decided to offer for Patty had come to naught. It took only a moment, however, for him to put thoughts of his sister aside and delight in the letter from Sir Charles Burroughs.

"It is from Charlie!'' he exclaimed, a grin on his face which reminded Daniel of how he looked as a schoolboy. The earl sobered as he read of his friend's wound.

"Are you inviting him to visit?"

"That is what I wished to talk to you about. Of course I would like to extend my hospitality, but since Serena has arrived, the only bedrooms I have available are small and sometimes damp in the winter." He paused, hoping Marcus would take the hint, but his friend only watched him intently. "I wondered if you might invite him to stay here with you. If it wouldn't be too much trouble, of course."

"Why, of course it would not. I'd be delighted, if you do not mind."

"No, not at all," Daniel replied, being ridiculously polite. "I daresay an eligible bachelor would find more of interest in your household than that of a vicar. Of course, Serena and I shall entertain him as often as possible. I should like Serena to become better acquainted with Charlie."

Marcus's eyebrows rose as he considered Daniel's words. Why, the sly fox: he intended to marry his sister off to Charlie Burroughs. Not a bad idea if it would succeed in removing the girl from his thoughts, surely, for she had taken up too much of his time as it was.

"Yes, I quite agree. After all, since there is such a shortage of eligible bachelors about, we shall want to do everything to please him," he replied with a friendly smile. "In fact, Patty wishes to have an entertainment for Miss Fenton. We shall include Charlie in our celebration, after he has recuperated a few

days. What do you say to that, Daniel? Give the ladies an opportunity to wear the ball gowns they are
so fond of."

"That will be quite wonderful," Daniel assured
him. Serena in evening dress would be sure to sway
Charlie and, perhaps, the man across from him, as
well.

"Well," Daniel said as he stood, suddenly anxious to be on his way, "that is settled. Please advise
me when Charlie is due to arrive, and I shall be on
hand to help you greet him. It has been an age since
I last saw him."

"Yes. It has been a full two years since I left him
in France." The earl followed the vicar to the door.
"Do you suppose he has changed much?"

"I doubt it. He was always a little bit on the go,
but probably he has matured since our school-days.
We certainly have." Suddenly, Daniel felt much older
than his twenty-eight years.

"Yes, of course. Will you join us for another cup
of tea?"

"No, if Serena is ready, I believe we shall go home.
I still have several chores to complete today. Thank
you again for agreeing to invite Charlie," he added,
as Marcus summoned Lawrence to request Miss
Fenton's presence.

"I shall be delighted to have him in my house. I
only hope his visit will accomplish what you are

seeking." Marcus studied the features of the man next to him.

"Oh, I am quite sure Charlie will recuperate nicely in the bosom of his friends."

"Of course, and it will enliven the social round here in the country to have an eligible bachelor about. Our parties will be the most popular."

Serena's arrival ended their conversation, and both men were grateful. Never had their words been so stiff and uncomfortable.

As she and her brother set out for the vicarage, Serena asked, "Is all well, Daniel?"

"Of course, my dear. Why do you ask?"

"You spoke privately with Lord Granville, and Patty seemed ... unhappy."

Daniel swung round sharply. "What do you mean?"

"Why, only that she seemed rather sad. She was about to perhaps confide in me, but I'm afraid Lord Granville and his brother entered at that moment, and she could not."

Daniel strode ahead, disturbed that he had caused Patty's unhappiness, unaware that he was outdistancing his sister until she called to him.

"Daniel, is this a race? Because I must tell you you are sure to win."

He grinned down at her. "No, my dear, I was only lost in thought. I set a furious pace when I have something on my mind."

"Is it what you were speaking to Lord Granville about?"

"No, that was a simple matter. A dear friend of ours requires a place to recuperate from his wounds. He wrote to enquire whether he might visit me at the vicarage, but I thought he would be made more comfortable at the big house."

"I do not wish to put you out, Daniel. I could move to a smaller room, truly. I do not mind."

He pulled his sister to him with one long arm. "Do not be silly, my dear. Actually, he is quite eligible and I . . . did not think it proper that he stay at the vicarage. Although it will be quite unexceptionable for you to enjoy his company at the big house."

"You are not matchmaking, are you, brother dear?"

"Of course not," Daniel said as he resumed his walking, staring straight ahead. "But with Charlie's arrival, there will be numerous parties for you to attend. And Patty, as well. I fear she works too hard and that she would do well to have some pleasure in life, also."

Serena thought of the happiness on Patty's face when she was in Daniel's company and wondered how an intelligent man like her brother could be such a slowtop. Before she could comment, however, Daniel continued.

"Lord Granville has promised an entertainment in honour of both of you after Charlie has had a few days to recuperate from his journey. Is that not thoughtful?"

Though she felt sure the idea for the entertainment had been suggested by Patty, Serena still felt rising excitement over the prospect of a party. She had attended few in London.

"That will be most diverting, Daniel. And I already have a lovely gown to wear, so you need not concern yourself with purchasing one for me."

"It never occurred to me to do so, my dear, but thank you for telling me."

Serena was relieved to see a smile return to Daniel's face, even if it was a half-hearted one. She vowed to learn tomorrow what had transpired between Daniel and Patty.

WHEN LORD GRANVILLE returned to the salon after the Fentons' departure, he discovered Augustus continuing to discuss the finer points of his stables and Patty staring vacantly, a glum expression on her piquant face.

"I am pleased you are finding much to amuse you about country life, Auggie," Marcus commented, smiling at his brother, "but I believe you have exhausted the topic of horses. Poor Patty looks almost asleep with ennui."

Augustus sank back, irritated with his brother's erroneous accusation and certain that Patty had enjoyed every moment of his discourse. He sipped his lukewarm tea in sullen silence.

Patty scarcely noticed the change in conversation.

"Patty? Is something bothering you?"

After repeating his query several times, Marcus leant over to touch his sister's hand. Jumping, she all but splashed her tea on the Aubusson carpet. "I am sorry. Did you wish something?"

"I spoke to you several times and you did not answer. Is something amiss?"

"No, of course not, Marcus. Do not be absurd." She set her cup on the tray and stood. "Well, I believe I shall retire for a while. My activities today have tired me."

Since Patty was customarily full of energy, Marcus found her comment even more alarming than her sad features. He followed her from the room. "Patty?" he called as she started up the stairs.

"Yes, Marcus?"

"If something is worrying you, you have only to tell me."

Patty blinked several times to hold back the sudden tears which welled in her eyes. "Thank you, Marcus, but . . . truly, there is nothing."

"Very well. Oh, I must warn you, we shall shortly be welcoming a house guest. An old friend from my school days as well as my regiment is recuperating from a wound and I have invited him to visit with us. You do not mind, do you?"

"No, of course not," she replied with little interest.

"If you do not object," Marcus added, hoping to pique his sister's interest and coax her from her blue devils, "we shall postpone the entertainment for Miss Fenton for a few days until Charlie has recovered from his journey and then he may join us."

"Very well."

Frustrated, Marcus watched her ascend the stairs, her shoulders slumped and her head bowed. He turned and went back into the salon.

"Auggie, do you know what is amiss with Patty?"

"No, but whatever it was, I am not the cause."

"I am not accusing you of anything, Auggie, but she seems distressed to me, and yet, she will not confide in me." Marcus paced the room, a frown on his face.

"She didn't say anything about being distressed. Usually I can tell when Patty's out of curl." He reached over for another macaroon.

"I can't help but feel that her depression of spirits is somehow connected to Daniel." Marcus ceased pacing, a forefinger thoughtfully stroking his bottom lip. "Come to think on it, Daniel himself seemed somewhat subdued. I suppose they may have had a quarrel."

"Why would she quarrel with the vicar? Seems like a nice enough chap."

Marcus observed his brother in some disgust. Auggie seemed to retain nothing in his head. When Miss Fenton returned in the morning, he would apply to her for information. She seemed a much more reliable observer than his brother.

CHAPTER SEVEN

"SHALL I make a separate list of expenses on the home farm, my lord?" Serena asked the next morning. Lord Granville had no more correspondence to be prepared.

"You do not mind?"

"No, of course not. I am here to assist you." She gathered a stack of papers and moved over to the table where she had worked the day before.

After a few minutes of silence, Lord Granville shifted in his chair. He cleared his throat several times until Serena looked up.

"Perhaps you would care for a cup of tea, Miss Fenton?" he asked. "I do not wish to tire you."

Puzzled, Serena said, "But I have worked less than an hour, my lord. There is no need to be concerned."

"I only thought...that is, I believe Patty is at home this morning and might enjoy your company."

He avoided her eyes, but she realized his offer must have been prompted by his concern for his sister. "I would be delighted to take tea with Miss

Browne, if you have nothing urgent you require me to do.''

"Good, good,'' Lord Granville said, rising from his desk. "I'll just ring for Lawrence and have him advise Patty you will be taking tea with her.''

Serena stacked up the papers on which she'd been working, and stood. "Will you be joining us, Lord Granville?''

"No, I must see Augustus about his survey of the home farm this morning. We shall take our tea in here.'' And that would keep his brother from intruding on the tête-à-tête he was creating, he added silently.

Nodding, Serena moved towards the door just as Lawrence opened it. Lord Granville quickly gave his instructions to the butler, and Serena prepared to follow him from the room.

"Oh, Miss Fenton,'' the earl called, stopping her. "I wondered—that is, Patty seems disturbed about something. If you could discover what is troubling her, without betraying her confidence, of course, I would appreciate it.''

His concern for his sister drew a warm smile from Serena, a gift she rarely bestowed upon Lord Granville. "I shall try to discover the problem, my lord.''

As she closed the door behind her, Lord Granville sat back down in his chair. The young lady's smile, combined with her vibrant beauty, was a dangerous weapon. It was a good thing Charlie was coming.

"THANK YOU for letting me join you, Patty," Serena said with a wide smile. "Your brother wished to interview Mr. Browne about the home farm."

"I'm delighted to have your company, Serena," Patty's words were all that was proper, but they lacked the spark which was usually present in her demeanour.

"Patty, what is the trouble? You look as though you'd lost your best friend."

Her eyes filled with tears and Patty clenched her fingers tightly together to keep from disgracing herself. "I think I have."

"What do you mean?"

"Last winter Daniel and I became the best of friends. I could share everything with him. Now . . . now he seeks excuses to avoid my company, and he doesn't talk to me about anything."

"Perhaps he is merely busy," Serena suggested, though she did not believe that was the problem.

"Forgive me, I should not be complaining to you of your brother. He . . . he is the finest man I know. I must accept the fact that he does not care for me as I care for him."

Patty's brave smile wrung Serena's heart. Though matrimony might not be her own choice, she believed both her brother and Patty would be happier in the married state. Why couldn't her brother see that?

"I still believe Daniel cares for you, Patty. Perhaps he does not believe you care for him."

A lone tear escaped and rolled down Patty's cheek. "I have done all but throw myself in his arms. He can have no doubt of my feelings."

Serena reached over to clasp Patty's hand in comfort. "Please do not give up, Patty. I want you for my sister. We should be such a happy family."

Even in her distress, Patty was mindful of Daniel's goal. "There is another way in which we could become sisters."

Serena, her thoughts on her brother and the young lady beside her, stared at her. "I beg your pardon?"

"We could become sisters if you were to marry my brother."

Laughter bubbled up in Serena. "You are absurd, Patty. Even if I were interested in marriage, and I am not, your brothers have no interest in me. The earl dismisses me for a hoyden, and Mr. Browne does not know that I exist. And will not unless I grow a mane and tail."

Patty's lips trembled into a smile at her friend's nonsense. "Auggie is rather taken with horses at the moment. But I am sure Marcus no longer thinks you improper. Last evening he said you were astoundingly efficient."

"How kind. I do not believe that is a recommendation for marriage, however. And since I am not a supporter of that institution, I believe it would be better for you to marry Daniel.''

"I am perfectly willing. It is Mr. Fenton who resists.'' Patty's sigh was long and deep.

"Then we must contrive something which would bring him round. What shall it be? You say he is avoiding you?''

"Yes. I am to teach the knitting class this afternoon. It is held at the vicarage and Daniel always spent a little time with us last winter. This morning I received a note informing me that he will be unavailable but that I should carry on. Yesterday, he escaped my presence as soon as possible.''

"Then we shall plan an outing which he must attend.''

Patty peeped at her friend from beneath her lowered lashes. "I know a way to ensure his presence.''

"How so?''

"You may not care for it.'' Patty waited for Serena's permission before continuing. "Daniel . . . Daniel has hopes of your marrying, and he will join us if it means you will have an opportunity to be accompanied by an eligible bachelor.''

"I know he hopes I shall marry, but as I have no intention of fulfilling his hopes, I don't wish to encourage him. Besides, we would have to locate an eligible bachelor who would not be heartbroken if I were to show no interest whatsoever in him.''

"I know of one," Patty inserted, enthusiasm colouring her voice.

With a chuckle, Serena guessed, "You are thinking of your brother." At Patty's nod, she continued, "Mr. Browne would not notice—"

"No! Not Auggie. Marcus. That is the brother I meant."

"The earl?" Serena's brows rose even as she giggled at the absurdity of the suggestion. "Daniel would not be fooled, Patty. Everyone knows how your brother detests me. Even Mr. Browne would be a better choice than the earl."

"That is the beauty of my plan. Auggie would not understand what was afoot, but Marcus knows I am in love with Daniel, and he has promised to do whatever I request within reason to help me attach Daniel's heart."

"But there must be another way," Serena protested.

"I can think of no other," Patty assured her, pleading with her eyes. "Daniel will only attend out of duty for his position or for his responsibility to you. And I can think of nothing which would ensure his presence because of duty as vicar. Unless I were on my deathbed," she added contemplatively. "No, I would not be able to fool him."

"No, I think not," Serena agreed drily.

"Then you will agree?"

Serena sighed. "Patty, you are forever talking me into—are you sure your brother will understand? I could not bear it if he thought I was pursuing him."

"Oh, Serena, you are a wonderful friend. Of course he will understand. I shall explain everything to him. Now, what shall we plan?"

"I suppose we could have a picnic. Are there any old ruins nearby? We could visit them on the pretext that I have never seen them."

"Yes, of course. There is a deserted abbey only an hour's drive from here, Oldham Abbey. Oh, what a marvellous idea, Serena. And if the weather tomorrow is as fine as today's, it would be—"

"Are you enjoying yourselves?" Marcus asked, walking into the back parlour. He immediately noted Patty's flushed cheeks and sparkling eyes and threw a look of gratitude to Serena.

"Oh, Marcus, Serena has had the most wonderful idea. We are to go on a picnic to Oldham Abbey."

"Very well. I can spare her a few hours. But be sure to take several footmen along for propriety," he warned, an indulgent smile on his face.

Serena stirred uneasily. The explanation might be awkward if Patty had not been completely honest.

"No, Marcus, you shall accompany us...and Daniel, as well."

"But, Patty, I have—"

"If you do not accompany us, Daniel will not." The light died in Patty's eyes. "He is avoiding me, you see."

Both young ladies watched the gentleman closely.

"Ah, then I shall enjoy visiting the abbey again. When do we go?" His immediate capitulation drew an enthusiastic hug from Patty and a look of amazement from Serena.

"Tomorrow, if the weather is as fine as today. Will you pen Daniel a note?"

Lord Granville's eyebrow rose in surprise. "You do not wish to invite him yourself?"

"He will refuse me, and I'm sure he will find some excuse should Serena ask him, but he cannot refuse you."

"And I thought you were so confident of Daniel," Marcus murmured. "Very well," he continued, holding up his hand when Patty would have protested. "I'll pen a note begging his appearance tomorrow, and Serena will deliver it when she returns to the vicarage."

"You are the best of brothers!" Patty exclaimed, giving him another hug.

Marcus returned the hug. "I am becoming quite accustomed to your throwing yourself at me, Patty. If only it didn't make Augustus suspicious."

Patty's delightful gurgle of laughter was Marcus's reward for his teasing. Over his sister's shoulder, he smiled at Serena. She had more than fulfilled his expectations. "How will you occupy yourself today?" he asked his sister as she pulled out of his arms.

With her natural exuberance restored, Patty said, "Oh, I have several tasks to complete before luncheon, and afterwards, I am resuming the knitting class at the vicarage. Serena, you must see the beautiful yarn I bought yesterday."

"Your brother is waiting for me to return to work, Patty. Perhaps I may see it later."

"I can spare you a few more minutes, Miss Fenton. You may return to the study when you and Patty have finished your visit."

"Very well, my lord. You are most generous." His kindness to his sister stirred Serena's heart. She quickly withdrew her gaze from him and turned to Patty.

The two girls linked arms and hurried from the room. Patty's laughter floated behind her, and Marcus smiled as he heard it. Yes, Miss Fenton had done an excellent job this morning.

DANIEL SAT at the rough-hewn table and chatted amiably with the elderly man across from him. Knitting class would have already begun, he knew, because Patty was always punctual. His mind wandered from the old man's tale, heard several times before, as he pictured Patty and her ladies, knitting needles flying, as they discussed many different subjects of concern.

Patty did as much good with her discussions as she did with her knitting lessons. The ladies would bring their problems to her for practical assistance, whether it was making their bread rise or disciplining their children. The only time he had discovered Patty at a loss was a marital difficulty one lady wished to discuss.

He smiled as he thought of her embarrassed confusion. She was such a darling!

"Vicar, how kin ye smile 'bout such an awful thing?"

"Sorry, Jasper," Daniel said hurriedly, "I was thinking of another difficulty I have." He rose. "Will you forgive me if I return another day to continue our conversation?"

"Course I will. Maizie says I talk too much, anyways." He rubbed the side of his wrinkled face. "She puts a right store in those knitting sessions. Right glad she was when Miss Browne came back. Fine woman, Miss Browne."

"Yes, she is, and most generous with her time."

"Make a good vicar's wife, Maizie says."

With a silent groan, Daniel forced himself to smile politely. "She would make an excellent wife for any man."

He swiftly bade the old man goodbye and began the walk back to the vicarage. He must not hurry, he reminded himself. After all, he had planned to absent himself for the entire duration of the knitting class. He should have remained with Jasper another half hour.

In spite of his intentions, his feet sped along the path and when he arrived back at the vicarage, the ladies still filled his parlour, their fingers moving quickly at their task.

"Good afternoon, ladies," he said as he entered the room. Patty kept her gaze on her knitting, but her cheeks turned bright red at his appearance, and all the ladies took note of it.

In only a matter of minutes, the knitting was stored away and Daniel found himself alone with Patty.

"I wished to tell you that...that I have planned an outing for Serena and Marcus tomorrow to the Oldham Abbey. I carry a note from Marcus to you which will explain. But you and I must accompany them, for they cannot go alone."

She would not look at him. With great dedication, she busied herself restoring the parlour to its pristine state.

Daniel considered her words. He had intended to avoid her, but it was important for Serena and Marcus to spend time together. When Charlie arrived, he hoped Marcus would already have an interest in Serena.

"It is kind of you to assist me, Patty. I shall look forward to our outing. Serena does not object?"

"She wishes to become familiar with the area, since it is to be her home. Perhaps I made the abbey sound more exciting than it is, but she will not know that until we arrive. And I'm sure she will be too polite to complain about the insignificance of our only ruin."

"We shall certainly hope so. I would like Marcus to see her on her best behaviour."

"They are working well together. Last evening at dinner, Marcus said she is very efficient." Patty peeped up at Daniel, her eyes hungry for the sight of him.

"'Efficient' does not seem a very romantic description," Daniel complained, thinking that he had never thought of Patty in such terms, in spite of her many talents.

Patty grinned at him. "No, but it is an improvement over his first impression of her."

Their shared laughter broke down the stiffness Daniel had so carefully constructed, and he drew back at once, recognizing danger.

Turning from her, he asked, "How did the class go on?"

Patty ached from wanting to reach out to him, but she bent to gather her belongings. "Fine."

"Jasper says Maizie sets great store by them."

"I am not surprised. I think it is the only time she is able to sit down. She works far too hard."

"There has been no word of Peter?" Maizie's husband was a soldier in the army and had not been home in six years. The woman struggled to care for her two children and her father-in-law.

"No. She grows discouraged at times. I have promised to write a letter to Peter on her behalf. He cannot read, but she hopes he will find someone to read it to him." She turned to look at Daniel. "Could we not start classes to teach at least the children to read?"

"You already do too much, Patty," Daniel said gently. "And there is the Dame's School in the village."

"But Maizie cannot afford to send her children there. And besides, she should learn to read herself."

Patty's fierce determination showed through her words, and Daniel grinned. "Now you are beginning to sound like those bluestockings in London, professing women's rights."

"Good. Perhaps I shall persuade Serena to join with me. We shall set the county on its ear."

Daniel shuddered at the thought. "Please, Patty, do not encourage Serena to go beyond what is proper. She is too often outrageous on her own."

Patty stared at her beloved in frustration. "I do not think you appreciate Serena at all."

Daniel only smiled. "It is your brother we must cause to appreciate Serena. I already am quite fond of her. She does not need your protection."

IN SPITE OF a foreboding that rain would ruin their plans, Patty discovered the sun shining and a beautiful day at hand when she arose the next morning, almost as if it were early September rather than October.

Her plans were almost overset when Auggie decided to join them, anxious to try the paces of a gelding he especially liked. Marcus requested that he ride to the north and inspect a tenant's barn, however, apologizing for forcing him to miss their outing.

"I do not mind, really. A ride is all I wanted. Will Murchison accompany me?"

"I think you can manage this on your own, Auggie. Murchison is busy, and he was most impressed with your knowledge the other day."

Augustus's chest swelled with pride. It was not often in the past two years that he had done anything to earn his brother's approbation. "Of course I can manage. I might stop for luncheon in the village on my way back. 'Twould make a nice change."

"An excellent idea," Marcus agreed. "Then I shall not feel such remorse for having robbed you of a social outing."

"Don't give it another thought. I'm not much at doing the pretty for the females, you know. And Patty won't miss me, will you, my dear?''

"Of course I shall," Patty assured her brother, "but I am proud of how much you are assisting Marcus." She held her breath until he beamed at her and reiterated his desire to inspect the barn.

Once Auggie was dispatched, Patty dressed in her new riding habit of blue velvet with dashing gold braid trim. It was the newest fashion in London and Daniel had never seen her in it.

Her riding hat sported two blue plumes and her dark hair was braided in a coil at the nape of her neck. She surveyed herself in the looking-glass and was satisfied. After all, she would never be tall and slender like Serena. Once, however, when she had complained about her lack of stature to Daniel, he had assured her he thought her the perfect size.

With a sigh, she left her room. If only he still felt that way.

Marcus was waiting for her in the entry hall. They were providing mounts for Daniel and Serena, so they set out for the vicarage, leading the other two horses, followed at a discreet distance by the servants who would lay out the picnic.

When they reached the vicarage, Daniel and Serena came out at once, pleasing Marcus. He disliked his animals to be kept standing. The little mare he had chosen for Serena seemed well suited to her, and he signalled for her to ride beside him as they set out for Oldham Abbey.

With a look over his shoulder at the second pair, he murmured to Serena, "I thought we would ride together to give the others a chance to converse."

"Of course," Serena agreed. "However, Daniel was not in a cheerful mood last evening. I only hope Patty is not disappointed."

When they were at least halfway to the Abbey, Serena and Marcus, who had discovered several enjoyable topics of conversation, were surprised to discover Patty insisting they change partners.

"I would like to ride with Serena the rest of the way," she said firmly, avoiding Daniel's gaze.

"Very well," Marcus agreed, though he watched Serena manoeuvre her mount back behind him with regret. He had found the young woman to be remarkably well-informed.

Once they were on their way again, Serena leaned towards Patty. "Is aught the matter?"

"No, of course not. It is just that Daniel will speak of nothing of interest to me. When he spoke at all, his words were all in praise of his friend, Sir Charles Burroughs. The man has not even arrived yet, and I am already tired of *dear Charlie!*"

CHAPTER EIGHT

As PATTY CONTINUED to complain of Mr. Fenton's standoffish air, Serena noted how easily Lord Granville sat his horse, even though he had to hold the reins in his left hand. He was a powerful man, commanding because of his size, but also because of his proud carriage.

"Serena? Serena!" Patty repeated, her eyes on her companion. "What are you thinking of? I have been talking to you and you do not answer."

Her cheeks red, Serena mumbled an excuse and turned her attention to Patty. "Are we almost there? I know it is indelicate to say so, but I am famished."

"Yes, it is only over the next hill. But I daresay we have misjudged the situation. It is clear Daniel wishes nothing to do with me."

"Then why does he constantly turn in his saddle and check our progress?"

Patty's gaze flew to the two men in front of them. "Does he? I hadn't noticed. I didn't wish him to think he mattered a jot to me."

Serena laughed at her friend just as the two men

moved back alongside them, ending their conversation.

"You are enjoying your ride?" Marcus asked, smiling at the two young ladies.

"Yes, it is a lovely day, quite warm for October," Serena responded.

"Miss Browne, you are comfortable?" Daniel asked, pretending a concern just to draw her gaze his way.

Patty flashed an angry glare at him and stared pointedly at her mount's ears. Marcus sought to alleviate the tension. "Daniel, we are among friends. I believe it would be appropriate for you to address Patty by her Christian name."

"You address Serena as Miss Fenton, do you not?" Daniel challenged.

Lord Granville was feeling quite in charity with Miss Fenton since she had pried Patty from her melancholy and organized his work, as well. Besides, she was a beautiful young woman and perhaps he'd been somewhat precipitate in his early condemnation of her. Today, she was a pattern card of propriety.

"I have not known your sister as long as you have Patty," he reminded his friend, "but if she has no objection, I should be honoured to call her by her given name."

"Of course, my lord," Serena coolly replied. In spite of their enjoyable ride, she found him a trifle overpowering and was reluctant to let him draw closer.

Lord Granville nodded and rode ahead to speak to the servants, accompanied by Daniel. Patty slumped in her saddle, her chin buried in the collar of her riding habit.

"Patty, you must not wear your heart on your sleeve so." When the other young lady turned to stare at her, Serena added, "Whether you and Daniel come to terms or not, you must have your pride."

"What use is pride if I must live without Daniel?" Patty muttered.

"For one thing, it improves your posture. You are sitting your horse like a sack of potatoes," Serena teased, though her description was accurate.

A smile broke through Patty's gloom, and she stiffened her spine. "You are right, Serena. What a good friend you are."

They soon joined the two gentlemen and the servants. Serena viewed the offerings sent from Lord Granville's kitchen appreciatively. A groom held her horse's head as she dismounted and led both her and Patty's horses away. Not far off some stone walls, half tumbling down, rested in the shade of several tall oaks.

"Is that Oldham Abbey?"

"Yes, it is not large, but I thought it would serve our purposes." Patty watched Serena, wondering if she would scorn their only ruin.

"It is charming. I can't wait to explore it. Oh, look, there is a stream nearby, also." Serena wandered in the direction of the brook, its noisy gurgle telling of its swift movement over rocks.

Lord Granville followed his secretary. "Do you wish to explore before luncheon?" he asked.

"Not really. I was just attracted to the stream," she assured him with a smile. Turning, she retraced her footsteps to the cloth spread on the grass and covered with an array of appetizing dishes. Soon they were all seated, the attendants serving them.

"The ride must have sharpened my appetite," Lord Granville confessed as he took another serving of the roasted quail. "Food always tastes better in the open air."

"Yes, it does," Daniel agreed.

"Are we allowed to enter the abbey?" Serena asked, her eyes on the old building.

"Parts of it are safe for exploration," Marcus assured her. "I shall be glad to guide you through it after luncheon."

Patty looked doubtfully at the ruins. "I do not like it. I think it is sad."

"I prefer the fresh air myself," Daniel added. "Perhaps you would like to remain here and oversee the cleaning up from luncheon. I shall offer my assistance."

Though all four knew there would be little work for Patty to do, each, for his own reasons, agreed to the arrangement. When they had finished their repast, Lord Granville assisted Serena to her feet and they strolled in the direction of the ruin, leaving Patty and Daniel at ease on the ground.

"Is your brother firmly set against matrimony?" Marcus murmured as he assisted Serena over a pile of stone which had fallen.

"I do not think so, though he will not discuss Patty with me," she added.

"He is a fine man, and I have no qualms about Patty's marrying him. But I do not wish her to harass him. In addition to being a fine vicar, he is my friend, and I would not betray him in that manner."

Serena liked the earl's words. His concern for her brother was admirable and the praise justified. "I make no doubt that he cares for Patty. But for some reason, he will not offer for her. Patty and I thought it might help if they spent more time together, but this morning seems not to have gone as well as we had hoped."

"Yet he seemed willing to be alone with her just now."

Serena feared she knew why her brother had been so agreeable, but she didn't intend to tell her companion. "How old is the abbey?" she asked, hoping to draw Lord Granville's thoughts away from her brother's behaviour.

"Hmmm? Oh, about five hundred years old."

Recalled to his role of tour guide, Lord Granville pointed out what little was known about the abbey, and Serena listened appreciatively. Having such a willing audience increased the earl's enjoyment of the afternoon.

When they returned to the site of the picnic, all the food had been cleared away, but the vicar and his companion were sitting far apart. Patty was industriously knitting and Daniel was staring across the grassy meadow.

The earl leaned over and murmured to Serena, "Why do you not invite Patty for a stroll? I believe I shall talk to the vicar. It is time to stop coddling those two."

Serena wasn't sure the earl's plan was a good one, but she had no alternative but to agree. When they reached the others, she said, "The abbey is charming, Patty. I'm so pleased you suggested our coming."

Patty smiled briefly, nodding in answer, and returned her attention to her knitting.

"Wouldn't you like to stroll about before we remount?" Serena asked. "I would love a closer look at the stream."

"Very well," Patty agreed. There was no enthusiasm in her voice, but she rose willingly.

The two ladies strolled over to the brook and began walking alongside it.

"I gather you made no progress with Daniel," Serena finally said.

"There is no progress to be made," Patty replied in clipped tones. "It is as I surmised. Your brother has no romantic interest in me."

"But—"

"No, Serena. I appreciate your concern, but I shall not pursue Daniel. It is as Marcus said: I must not make him uncomfortable here. He is a wonderful vicar."

They continued their walk in silence, Serena unable to find any response to Patty's conclusion. Perhaps the earl would have more success.

When they came to a wide, shallow area of the stream, with large rocks lining the edge, Patty suggested they rest for a few moments. Serena agreed and they each chose a flat rock in the sunshine.

"It is amazingly warm for October, is it not?" Serena asked. "If you do not mind, I believe I shall remove my jacket."

"I shall also. Mine is snug after that huge meal," Patty complained. Their muslin blouses were much more appropriate for the weather than the heavy velvet. The magic of a beautiful afternoon outdoors began to ease some of the distress Patty felt, and she relaxed.

Serena, watching the swift flow of the stream, turned to Patty. "The water is quite shallow here. I believe I'll wade in it."

"What? You mean actually put your boots in the water?"

"No, silly. I shall remove my boots and stockings. Have you never waded in water? It is a glorious feeling, even if the water is cold. It will refresh you before we make our return ride."

Patty stared as Serena prepared herself for her entrance into the stream. "You are serious?"

"Of course I am. You should try it, Patty."

"You have done this before?"

"Yes, there was a stream near our home. Daniel let me wade with him when I was a child. He would not teach me to swim, however," she grumbled, a long-held resentment colouring her words. "He said proper ladies do not swim."

In spite of her anger towards Daniel, Patty had great respect for the vicar's opinion. If wading was acceptable, it sounded too delicious to refuse. She immediately began pulling off her riding boots.

Soon the two young ladies were giggling and splashing in the water, their skirts held up in their hands.

"Wading is so refreshing!" Patty exclaimed, her delight in the day restored. "I—" With a piercing scream as she lost her footing, she fell forward into a deeper pool of water than either of them had been prepared for.

AROUND THE BEND in the stream and out of sight, Lord Granville had been leading up to questions about the vicar's personal feelings about his sister. But he discovered that broaching such a subject, even with a close friend, or perhaps especially with a close friend, was not easy.

"I am looking forward to Charlie's arrival," he began.

"Yes," Daniel said. "It will be good to see him again."

"I wonder if he has married," Marcus murmured, his eyes fixed sharply on Daniel.

There was a frown on Daniel's face as he sat up straighter. "Surely he would have mentioned such a thing in his letter?"

"Not necessarily. After all, it was a brief letter. Does it upset you to think he may have married?"

"No, of course not," Daniel said, though he would regret not having Charlie as a spur to Marcus's interest in Serena.

"It changes one's life, I've heard, to enter the state of matrimony."

"Yes."

"Do you ever contemplate doing so?"

"Yes, I intend to take a wife," Daniel said cautiously, wondering why his friend would ask such a question—unless he himself was contemplating matrimony. Would Serena be his chosen bride?

Daniel's response left Marcus at *point non plus*. If his friend contemplated marriage, it must not be Patty whom he hoped to marry, or he would already have asked for her hand. Unhappily, he considered his sister's future.

In the silence which had fallen, a scream rent the air. Immediately, both men leapt to their feet.

"That is Patty!" Daniel shouted and ran in the direction of the sound, Marcus at his heels.

They arrived at their destination in time to see the two young ladies struggling from the stream, their clothing soaked. Unfortunately, the muslin blouses, when wet, were as invisible as the wind, revealing the young ladies' charms for all to see.

Though stunned, Marcus had the presence of mind to turn and dismiss the three servants who had followed them. He only hoped the distance had denied them a clear picture of what *he* saw.

Daniel assisted the two young women the last few steps from the water and immediately handed them their jackets. "Put these on at once."

"But Daniel, we are wet. It will ruin—"

"Do as I say, Serena!" he snapped, in an imperious tone utterly unlike his usually gentle demeanour.

Both men avoided looking at the two young ladies, though each of them found their first view of one of the young ladies had been firmly implanted in his mind.

"How did this occur?" Marcus demanded grimly, his brain valiantly fighting its preoccupation. "Surely you did not fall in?" His question had scarcely left his lips when he noted the bare toes sticking out from beneath the velvet skirts heavy with water. "Patty?" he demanded ominously.

"W-W-We—" Patty began, shaking not only from the chill, but also from fright at the anger on her brother's face.

Serena took pity on her friend. "It is my fault. I induced Patty to wade in the stream with me."

"You intentionally entered the stream?" Marcus roared, stunned by such behaviour.

"My lord," Daniel intervened, "I believe questioning should wait. It would be best if we set out on our return journey as soon as possible so that the young ladies might remove their wet clothing."

Marcus glared at his friend but nodded in agreement.

"Serena, Marcus and I will return for the servants and horses. While we are gone, wring out the water from your skirts as much as possible and then put your stockings and boots back on." He avoided looking at Patty entirely, and her heart sank.

"Yes, Daniel," Serena agreed, her voice subdued. She knew she had displeased her brother considerably.

"And you must hurry. We won't be gone long, and the servants have already seen more than is proper."

His words caused the vicar considerable embarrassment, and he avoided looking at the ladies or Lord Granville as he hurried in the direction of their original stopping place.

Without a word, Lord Granville followed him. All his early doubts about Miss Fenton came back as he returned to the servants and horses. Her behaviour was unacceptable and a bad influence upon his sister. Never would Patty have done such a thing until Serena Fenton arrived.

Serena wasted no time. As soon as the men were a short distance from them, she gathered her skirt in her hands and began wringing the water from it. "Patty, please hurry. They are angry enough as it is. We do not dare to keep them waiting."

"Y-yes. They will never forgive us," Patty wailed even as she followed Serena's example.

"Lord Granville will forgive you, Patty. After all, I explained it was my fault."

"But we both know I wanted to enter the stream, and I shall not lie about it to Marcus. It was my stupid carelessness that caused the difficulty."

"I should have warned you to be careful where you stepped." She tried to reach the back of her skirt and could not. "Patty, if you will wring out the back for me, I shall do the same for you. I wish we had not had to put on our jackets so soon. It would not have taken our blouses long to dry out."

"Perhaps we should take them off now and then put them back on when they return."

"A good idea," Serena agreed. She stripped off her jacket before turning to assist Patty.

"Serena!" Patty almost screamed.

"What is the matter?"

"I can see through your blouse. It is almost as if you were unclothed." The realization that their nakedness had been the reason for Daniel's abrasiveness struck both young ladies at the same time.

Though her cheeks were flaming, Serena shook her head. "You might as well remove your jacket. The blouses will dry out quickly. There is little we can do about the earlier event."

"I th-think I shall die of embarrassment," Patty whispered as she stood for Serena to remove most of the water from her skirt.

Serena turned her back to Patty for her assistance. "They are both gentlemen. I'm sure they will not mention what has occurred."

"Marcus may not say anything about our . . . our nakedness, but he will have a great deal to say about my wading," Patty said mournfully.

"You must place the blame on me, Patty. He will believe you."

"No, no, I must be honest." They both sat down to put on their stockings and boots. After a moment of silence, Patty added, "And if I am honest, Serena, I must confess I enjoyed it immensely. Until I fell, of course.''

''Men are allowed to swim. I do not understand why we are not. Though I have heard of bathing machines in Bath.''

''What are they?''

''They are small shelters which are dipped in the ocean to allow one to go into the water. It sounds very strange, but I am determined to try one if ever I visit Bath.''

''I shall never be allowed to go anywhere once Marcus returns. My punishment will be banishment to my room for the rest of my life.''

''Even Lord Granville would not be that cruel, Patty,'' Serena assured her, hoping she was right. The sound of horses' hooves brought the two young women to their feet, pulling down their still-wet skirts and shrugging into their jackets.

As the riders appeared round the bend, they finished their fastenings and breathlessly turned to wait for their escorts.

The two men dismounted and Lord Granville signalled for the servants to ride on. Each man turned to his own sister to assist her mounting. As soon as the ladies were settled in their side-saddles, the men remounted and the horses were turned towards home without a word being spoken.

It was an uncomfortable ride for the two ladies. Their wet habits made it a chilling experience, and

Patty leant towards Serena to whisper, "I believe I shall have blisters in unmentionable places when we finally reach home."

Serena could only nod in agreement. The two men rode ahead of them and ignored their existence, which was something of a relief to both young ladies.

Their outing had been a miserable failure, Serena realized. Daniel had appeared even more withdrawn from Patty, and after she had convinced Patty to wade, Daniel might even think Patty was not fit to be a vicar's wife. She would be sure to explain to Daniel that it had been all her fault.

Patty could not forget that Daniel had seen her almost naked. It would be difficult to face him ever again. Not that she would have the opportunity: Marcus was sure to exact punishment.

Marcus rode with his eyes fixed straight ahead. He had recognized Serena's beauty when he first saw her, and the good impression she had made the past few days had wiped away his earlier opinion about her deportment. But today he was reminded of why he should not be trapped by her beauty: an earl's wife would never behave as she had today. And he would put the picture he had of her walking out of the stream completely out of his mind—at least he would try.

Daniel felt weary. The day had been difficult enough before the accident, as he attempted to avoid a confrontation with Patty. And now he had to fight not only his inclinations, but his imagination, as well. After all, visions of Patty, her blouse wet, were not proper for a vicar.

CHAPTER NINE

A MESSAGE WAS RECEIVED from Granville House the following morning, advising them of the earl's absence, which eliminated the need for Miss Fenton to assist him.

Serena read the message and then passed it on to her brother. After reading it, he said briskly, "It is just as well. With the cold you have this morning, bed is the best place for you."

"It is not serious," Serena said dismissively. Her brother had been quite gentle last evening when he warned her about leading others astray. Serena had wished to enquire of him if the two gentlemen had seen their state of undress, but she was too embarrassed to raise the topic.

"Perhaps, but I think it best you remain indoors today and rest. I hope Miss Browne is not similarly afflicted."

"Will you call on her today, to be certain?" Serena asked.

"No," Daniel replied, his rosy cheeks reflecting his embarrassment. He could not think of Patty without remembering yesterday. "I have a great many tasks to accomplish today."

"If I pen her a note, may the stable lad deliver it for me?"

"Of course, my dear." Daniel hurriedly finished his breakfast and left the table.

"You would think I had the smallpox instead of a cold," Serena complained to herself. Daniel didn't seem overeager for her company, any more than Patty's.

After several hours alone, except for the occasional appearance of Mrs. Washburn to see to her needs, Serena was delighted to discover Patty had responded in person to her note.

"Are you all right?" her guest asked as she seated herself. "I would not have come, except that you said you were ill—and that Daniel would be out most of the day."

Serena, with a red nose and an eiderdown tucked round her, assured Patty she was quite well.

"It is just a cold. Daniel insists that I remain indoors, and I was lonely."

"That is wise." Patty twisted her hands in her lap before asking softly, "Was Daniel very angry?"

"No, he was kind, as always, which makes me feel all the worse for having disappointed him."

"Yes. Marcus was quite restrained. I did try to tell him that it was not your fault, Serena, but...but I'm not certain I was able to convince him." Patty sent a silent apology to her friend.

"Don't concern yourself, Patty. The earl did not consider me properly behaved before yesterday. And the accident was mostly my fault." Serena plucked at the coverlet restlessly. "Daniel has warned me several times to consider before I choose a path of behaviour which will cause difficulties. I forget."

"But they would never have known if I had watched where I was stepping. It is entirely my fault we got all wet."

"Never mind," Serena said. "At least you have not been confined to your room on bread and water." Her attempt at a smile was not terribly successful.

With a frown, Patty said, "No, Marcus offered me no punishment at all. I was quite surprised."

"Why did he leave for London?"

Patty groaned. "That is another strange event. I tried to explain what happened and Marcus suddenly said he had to go to London. When I asked him why, he said he wished to ensure Sir Charles a comfortable journey." She shrugged. "It seems that both Daniel and Marcus are looking forward to the man's visit much more than I."

Serena lay back against a pillow, suddenly tired. "Daniel said he is a good friend."

"I believe you have a fever," Patty said, leaning forward to place a cool hand against Serena's flushed cheek. "Yes, you do. Have you taken any medicine?"

"It is nothing which will not pass," Serena protested as Patty stood and made for the door. "Where are you going?"

"To send for the doctor and ask Mrs. Washburn for a cool drink for you."

"But, Patty—" Serena began but stopped when her guest disappeared from view. In truth she did not feel very well, but she was determined not to cause even more difficulties.

In only a short period of time, Serena was back in her bed, dressed in a fresh nightgown and sipping a glass of lemonade. Patty sat beside the bed to ensure that she followed directions.

"The lemonade is most refreshing."

"Yes. Barley water is commonly used, but it does not taste nearly as good. I prefer lemonade." She leaned over and wiped Serena's face with a cool, damp cloth. "I feel so responsible. If I had been more careful—"

"Do not be a goose, Patty," Serena said hoarsely. "I would probably have fallen ill anyhow. I should never have suggested wading." She gulped as her eyes filled with tears. "And now I shall cause Daniel more trouble. I should never have come to stay with him."

Patty handed her a handkerchief, recognizing her tears as those of weakness caused by her illness. Daniel, however, having been alerted by Mrs. Washburn of Serena's worsening condition, was greatly alarmed.

"Serena? Are you all right?" he demanded, bursting into the room. He drew up short for a moment to discover Patty with his sister, but the tears absorbed his attention. "Whatever is the matter? Why are you crying?"

Since Serena seemed incapable of answering, Patty said softly, avoiding his eyes, "She feels she is too much of a burden to you."

Daniel sat on the edge of the bed as Patty moved back and tenderly took his little sister in his arms. "Don't be absurd, my dear. I was much too lonely before you came to live with me."

His kind words released the torrents of her misery, and Serena pressed her face into his shoulder and sobbed. Patty decided brother and sister should have a few moments of privacy and went to the kitchen to await the doctor's arrival as well as to request some beef broth for Serena.

Doctor Capps's evaluation of Serena's condition only echoed what Daniel and Patty had surmised. She had a cold and had to remain warm and cosseted for a few days until she felt better. Daniel expressed his thanks and escorted the man to his buggy while Patty tried to tempt Serena with Mrs. Washburn's broth.

"But I am not hungry," she said fretfully.

"I know, my dear, but you must keep up your strength, or you will never get well. Try just a few sips."

Daniel returned in time to hear Patty's words. She was the best nurse in the county, and he could not ask for better care for his sister. But if Patty were to nurse, she would be constantly at the vicarage. Daniel shrugged. He would just have to withstand temptation for Serena's sake.

"You will help nurse her?" Daniel asked quietly as he came to stand beside Patty.

Though her cheeks turned bright red, she said, "Of course, if you will allow it."

"I would appreciate your assistance. Serena was always subject to high fevers when she was a child. I only hope she has a mild illness." He, too, encouraged Serena to swallow her broth, but when she had almost finished the bowl, she rebelled against taking another spoonful.

"You have been very good. Why do you not try to rest a little now, Serena, and I shall help Mrs. Washburn fix you an especially tempting dinner."

The patient groaned at the thought of any more food, but she turned on her side and snuggled into the pillow. Patty placed a fresh cloth on her forehead, and the two attendants withdrew to the hallway.

"Will Marcus object to your nursing Serena?"

"Of course he will not, Daniel. At any rate, he has gone to London to escort Sir Charles. I do not expect him to return for several days."

"How kind of Marcus to go to so much trouble for Charlie."

"It seems he is quite anxious for Sir Charles to visit," Patty replied, her lips twisted in irritation. "You must all have been quite good friends at school."

Daniel avoided her gaze. "Yes, of course. And it has been a long time since we've seen him." Marcus's actions made Daniel wonder again if Marcus was also matchmaking, only in Patty's interest rather than Serena's.

"Have you corresponded with Sir Charles through the years?"

"No, his letter was the first word I have had of him except for Marcus's visits with him on the Continent." Seeing the speculative look on Patty's face, Daniel decided it would be best to abandon Charlie as a topic of conversation. "Shall you remain with Serena for the afternoon? I must visit one of Marcus's tenant farmers. I understand he has been abusing his wife and—"

"It is all right, Daniel. I shall remain with Serena."

Daniel looked down into her blue eyes and desperately sought to remember the reasons he could not yet ask her to marry him. "Patty... Patty, you are such a dear and generous person. I... thank you."

"Serena is my friend, Daniel. I am delighted to assist her." She lowered her lashes to hide the emotion in her eyes. She wanted to assure Daniel that she would do anything to help him, but she did not believe he wanted to hear those words.

Daniel reached out and pressed her shoulder in gratitude before hurrying down the stairs.

FOR SEVERAL DAYS, a pattern of sharing the care for Serena was developed. Patty was beside her while Daniel carried out his duties. When he returned to the vicarage, Patty went home. Serena received excellent care, and Patty and Daniel spent no time together except for brief discussions about the patient.

On the fourth day, Serena was much improved and allowed to join the knitting session in Daniel's parlour. The vicar himself was absent, of course.

Though she did no knitting, Serena was able to observe how wonderful Patty was with the women. To think that Patty had feared she might replace her brought hastily subdued giggles to Serena's lips.

To cover her ill-placed amusement, she asked, "Patty, for whom are you knitting that scarf?"

There were many covert looks from the ladies in the circle as Patty's cheeks flamed. "I—I thought the Vicar could use a scarf. Even in the worst of weather he is out and about and . . . and I . . . my brothers do not require one as much.''

"How thoughtful of you,'' Serena said warmly, hoping to relieve Patty's embarrassment. "I am so terrible at knitting that Daniel has refused to wear my efforts. He will undoubtedly appreciate such a lovely scarf.''

"Miss Browne is very skilful,'' Maizie enthused. She was one of Patty's staunchest supporters.

"Yes, she is. I am afraid I do not have the patience to manipulate the needles as all of you do.''

"After ye recover, ye'd best learn,'' an older lady recommended, "so's you can attach a husband.''

Serena only nodded. She didn't intend to share her view of matrimony with the ladies of the neighbourhood. For once, she stopped and considered how those words might reflect on her brother.

"Reckon knittin's not what most men look for in a wife. It's just one of those extra things that women do,'' Maizie said. "My Peter didn't know and more like didn't care if'n I knew what a knittin' needle looked like when he wedded me.''

The ladies laughed and Serena and Patty joined in, even though their cheeks were red. "I believe I'd best see Miss Fenton back to bed now,'' Patty said, putting down her knitting. "She mustn't stay up too long.''

Serena made no protest. She was ready to escape

their company. With Patty beside her, she climbed the stairs and they entered Serena's bedchamber.

"Patty, I'm sorry I asked about your knitting. I did not intend to embarrass you."

"Don't worry. I'm afraid all the ladies know how I feel about Daniel. I cannot hide my feelings when he enters the room."

"Are their remarks always so...so..."

Patty came to her assistance. "Oh, yes. Sometimes even more so. Once, Mrs. Flannery asked me about...about the more intimate side of marriage. I was so embarrassed that I was unable to respond. Maizie offered a suggestion and the woman was satisfied, but I could not bear to look at any of them for the remainder of the afternoon."

"Thank goodness you are the one who faces them, because I could not. Besides, my knitting is dreadful." Serena smiled at Patty and squeezed her hand before lying down on the bed. "I am a little tired, after all. Will you come up after the ladies have departed?"

"Of course I shall."

Serena lay in the bed thinking about her friend. It was incredible that Patty was so well suited to the life of a vicar's life but Daniel could not see it. Something was not as it should be.

As her eyes were closing, snatches of remarks Daniel had made about Patty floated in her head. Suddenly her eyes flew open. Why had she not seen it before? The only complaint Daniel had made about Patty was her rank. He didn't think she should lower herself to marry a vicar.

Could that truly be the difficulty? How could Daniel think such a thing? Lord Granville was sometimes a little stiff with her, but never with Daniel. Serena puzzled over her thoughts. Perhaps Daniel's friendship with Lord Granville was part of the problem. She knew Daniel would never wish to take advantage of a friend. Did he think Lord Granville would hesitate to refuse his offer because of their friendship? Or that his rejection of Daniel's suit would affect his appointment?

Sure now that she had discovered the difficulty, Serena intended to think of a way to overcome it, but she fell asleep. When Patty crept into her room half an hour later, she discovered her deep in slumber.

Returning down the stairs, she met Daniel as he entered the vicarage.

"How is Serena?" he asked, the same question he had asked each day upon his return.

"Much better. She has scarcely any fever and has remained out of bed most of the day. She is sleeping now, however."

"Thanks to your good care, Patty. I thank you so much for your concern."

Patty shrugged. "I am pleased to assist her, Daniel. Well, I must be on my way. I ordered a room prepared for Sir Charles and I must see if my orders were carried out.''

''Your carriage has not yet arrived. Come and have a cup of tea.''

''Thank you, but I believe I shall walk. The exercise will do me good.'' Patty reached for her cloak, hanging near the door.

''We don't want you to fall ill, as well.''

''I shall not.'' She pulled her cloak around her, indicating her intentions.

''Then I shall join you,'' Daniel said impulsively.

''No, Daniel, because then you would have to walk back, and you have already been out a great deal today.'' Patty turned her face up to Daniel, concern in her eyes.

Smiling down at her sweetness, Daniel reminded her, ''I am not prone to illness, my dear. I am always out and about in the winter.''

He opened the door for her and the two of them walked out into the blustery wind of late fall. He stopped Patty and pulled her hood over her head before taking one of her small hands and pulling it through his arm.

After walking for several minutes in silence, he asked, ''How was the knitting class this afternoon?''

''Fine. Serena joined us for part of it.''

Daniel cleared his throat. ''I hope she didn't knit.''

''Why would you say that?''

"Because the last time she knitted, I was the recipient of her efforts."

Patty looked up at his grin and wanted to embrace him. "No, she did not knit," she assured him with a laugh. "I don't believe she has any interest in it."

"I am grateful for that."

They continued on, more at ease with each other than they had been since Patty's return from London. Daniel told her of the various families he'd visited that day and she asked questions and made comments.

Finally, Daniel asked, "Patty, my dear, was Marcus very angry with you about... about our picnic?"

She stumbled slightly at the change of subject. "No—no, he was not." She paused before adding, "I'm afraid he placed most of the blame on Serena, but, truly, Daniel, I tried to explain that it was entirely my fault."

He patted her hand. "I'm sure you did, my dear. Don't concern yourself about it. Serena should never have suggested such a thing."

"I do not see what was so wrong with it." She looked at Daniel from the corner of her eye to see if she had shocked him. "It felt wonderfully refreshing until I fell. I should like to go wading again."

"I would not express those sentiments to Marcus, if I were you," Daniel said drily.

"Did you condemn Serena for her actions?"

"No, of course not. But she should not have induced you to join her, and it would have been better if she'd waited until you were not with her."

"Do you truly know how to swim?"

Daniel raised his eyebrows. "Serena has been telling tales, I suppose?"

"She said men sometimes swam. I just wondered if you had done so?"

"Yes, I have, as has Marcus, but don't tell him I spoke to you of it." He could see more questions poised on Patty's lips and he hurriedly said, "I believe we'd best change the subject, my dear, or Marcus will be unhappy with both of us."

"I suppose so."

"When do you expect him to return?"

"He has been gone four days and it takes two days to reach London. He could return this evening, but I would not expect to see him until tomorrow or the next day. There is no reason for him to rush his journey."

"True. Charlie will probably need to travel slowly."

"How badly wounded is he?" Patty asked, for the first time showing interest in the man.

"I do not know. His letter was very brief. I hope he is not suffering from a serious wound. I think you'll enjoy his visit."

Patty could work up little enthusiasm for anyone or anything that might diminish her time with Daniel. "Perhaps his recovery will be swift. Then we can go ahead with our party for Serena and him."

"It is kind of you and Marcus to include Serena."

Pulling Daniel to a halt, Patty looked up into his eyes. "Even if we did not care for Serena, and we do, we would want to celebrate her arrival because of you, Daniel."

The love he saw in her eyes made his heart lurch. He raised her hand to his lips.

The sound of a carriage bowling along the road at a swift pace drew Daniel's attention away and Patty struggled to hide her disappointment.

Both turned to look down the road which led to the big house and discovered Marcus had made a very fast trip indeed.

"Do you suppose Sir Charles was not able to accompany Marcus back?" Patty asked with a frown.

"I don't know. Let's hurry and see."

The two quickened their pace and reached the front steps just as the earl's travelling carriage drew to a stop. Several footmen raced down the steps and the door was swung open. Marcus disembarked and stared at the large audience waiting to greet him.

"I did not expect such a reception, even for Charlie. Is everything all right?" he asked his sister.

"Serena has been ill and I've been nursing her each day. Daniel escorted me home today."

"Serena ill? Is it serious?" Both Daniel and Patty noticed that the always proper Lord Granville referred to the vicar's sister by her first name.

"No, not now. She has recovered nicely, thanks to Patty's excellent nursing. Did Charlie accompany you?"

"Is that Daniel?" a voice from inside the carriage called.

Daniel stepped over to the door and greeted the man inside before offering to help him out. In a moment, Patty was introduced to the now famous Charlie.

"How do you do, Sir Charles," she said to the blond man, a little shorter in stature than either the vicar or the earl, who slowly emerged from the carriage with a pleasant smile on his face.

"Marcus never told me his sister was a beauty, Miss Browne, or I would have visited his house much sooner." He attempted a bow but almost toppled over.

Marcus and Daniel lent him support on each side. "Always the ladies' man, Charlie. You'd best wait to display your charms until you have recovered," Daniel suggested with a strained laugh.

"Sorry, Miss Browne. Your beauty caused me to forget my difficulties."

"Such lovely words are more appreciated than a bow, Sir Charles. Welcome to Granville House."

She led the way into the house, followed by Sir Charles, supported by two very unhappy men.

CHAPTER TEN

IT WAS SEVERAL DAYS before Serena met Sir Charles Burroughs. Daniel decided she was not well enough to accept the invitation to dinner Lord Granville had immediately extended to them until then.

"You have not spent a great deal of time with your friend since his arrival," Serena commented as they travelled to Granville House in her brother's old tilbury.

"Well, I do have many duties," he reminded her, but Serena noticed his eyes did not meet hers.

Slipping her arm through his, she murmured, "You have devoted too much time to me. I have felt such a fraud the past few days. I should have been assisting you instead of demanding your time. Yours and Patty's. She was so faithful coming to visit each day. I'm surprised the earl allowed her to do so."

"I'm sure you are misjudging Marcus. He has seemed most anxious for you to return to health."

Serena said nothing. She was certain Daniel was exaggerating the earl's concern. "How goes Sir Charles's recuperation?"

"Very well, I believe. Patty said yesterday that his wound was not severe. Doctor Capps thought he would be completely recovered in a matter of weeks. As it is now, he limps and cannot remain on his feet for long periods of time."

"Well, I shall excuse you from now on to spend time with your friend. He would probably enjoy a game of chess in the evenings."

Daniel said nothing. In truth, he had avoided visiting Charlie because the man was not doing what he had wished him to do. Instead of flirting with Serena, an impossibility since he had not met her as yet, he flirted with Patty. After visiting at the big house the first evening of Charlie's arrival, Daniel had found it too painful to watch him attempt to win Patty's favour.

The tilbury drew to a halt before the front steps, and Daniel handed the ribbons over to a footman and assisted his sister himself to descend from the vehicle. "I feel I should have hired a grand carriage to convey you to dinner, my dear. You look exquisite this evening."

Serena sighed. "As much as Mildred vexed me, she was exceedingly generous with my wardrobe. But, since we were seldom invited anywhere, I had no place to wear such finery."

"Well, now that you move in elevated circles with your brother," he teased, puffing out his chest, "you will be able to display all your fine clothes. And I predict that in no time you will be snapped up in marriage."

"You are the one who should marry, Daniel," Serena said quite seriously. "There is too much work for you to attend to. A good wife would relieve you of some of your duties."

The door was opened and Daniel did not have an opportunity to reply. Lawrence led them to the formal salon and announced them.

Presented to Sir Charles Burroughs, Serena smiled and swept an elegant curtsy.

"My, do all the men in this county have beautiful sisters?" he demanded gallantly.

Augustus, having imbibed rather generously before dinner, pondered his question seriously. "No, don't think so. Some don't have sisters at all, and some of them—"

"Auggie, I believe Charlie was offering a compliment to Miss Fenton, not asking about the other young ladies in the county." Marcus bowed his apology for his brother's response to the ladies.

It was his first real look at Miss Fenton dressed in her London best, and he held his breath. She wore a foam-green silk gown, its modest neckline still exposing much of her creamy skin. A darker green ribbon pulled the dress taut beneath her breasts, the sight of which, unfortunately, reminded him dramatically of their picnic. He swiftly offered his guests a sherry, hoping to distract his errant thoughts.

Sir Charles sat on the sofa with a beautiful young lady on each side of him and regarded his friends with some puzzlement. He was delighted to see both Marcus and Daniel, but their behaviour was most confusing.

All the way from London, Marcus had spoken about the vicar's sister, Miss Fenton. He had offered a glowing description of her charms, to the point that Charlie believed the man to be besotted with the young lady.

During the little time he'd spent with Daniel, the vicar, too, spoke of Miss Fenton, though his eyes always followed Miss Browne. He also included praise of Miss Browne's kind heart and generous works. Charlie was delighted that his friend had found a young lady so suited to the demands of being a vicar's wife, and Marcus had found a beautiful woman to fill the role of an earl's wife.

He had seen nothing to gainsay his thoughts, including the responses of the two ladies to the men who admired them. Neither man, however, had made his feelings public, apparently, and Charlie wondered why not. Anxious not to offend either man, Charlie flirted with both Serena and Patty, hoping to convey his approval to both friends.

Marcus and Daniel watched the ongoing entertainment with outward smiles and inward groans. Daniel hadn't intended to enmesh Patty in Charlie's web of charm, while for his part, Marcus awakened to the possibility of marrying his sister to Charlie, then dismissed it. She loved Daniel, and until he rejected her, she would never look at another man; besides, he counted on Charlie to remove the temptation of Miss Fenton from his reach. Augustus was completely oblivious to any difficulties.

After dinner, they returned to the salon, joining the ladies at once.

"Miss Browne, why do you not play for Sir Charles," Daniel suggested. That would put some distance between Patty and his friend.

Patty demurred. "I have not practiced in weeks, Mr. Fenton. It would be painful to listen to me play. Serena, would you care to..."

With a grimace, Serena said, "I am almost as accomplished at the pianoforte as I am at knitting, Patty."

Patty and Daniel both chuckled, but the others stared at Serena blankly. She explained, "I am a total loss at both of those womanly skills."

"But she is exceptionally well educated for a woman," Marcus hurriedly said. Serena stared at him in surprise, as did several others in the room. "She has been of great assistance since I, er, had this accident," he added, waving his bandaged wrist at Charlie.

"You never told me how you managed to injure yourself, Marcus," Charlie noted.

There was an awkward pause before several people rushed to fill it. Patty, Marcus and Serena all stopped in confusion, but Serena continued before the other two could do so. "I'm afraid I am the culprit, sir. I—I fell from a tree and Lord Granville broke my fall. I escaped injury, but he unfortunately did not."

"How gentlemanly of you, Marcus," Charlie commented, ignoring the outrageousness of the situation.

"Miss Fenton fails to mention that she was trying to rescue a kitten for a young boy. It was a most courageous effort."

"That's not what you said that day," Augustus remarked, surprised at his brother's defence of a young lady he had described as a hoyden. "You said—"

"Augustus! I believe enough has been said on the subject. I never discovered how you fared in your inspection of that barn."

As a conversational gambit, a tenant's barn was not particularly successful, though Augustus remembered a horse he'd seen in the village which kept him talking for quite some time.

Patty turned the conversation to the entertainment they planned as soon as Auggie paused to draw a breath. "Have you any preference as to the type of entertainment, Sir Charles? Of course, dancing is ruled out since your injury will not have progressed to that extent, but we might play cards or simply invite several neighbours over for an evening of music.''

''Do not rule out dancing. I may not be able to participate, but I enjoy watching it.''

''We would not wish you to feel left out, sir,'' Patty said uncertainly, looking to her brother for guidance.

''Nonsense.'' Sir Charles spoke before Marcus could. ''It would do my heart good to watch the young ladies being swung about the room. As I remember, Marcus and Daniel were quite accomplished dancers.''

The two young ladies looked at their brothers in surprise.

''Capital idea,'' Auggie added. ''Saw a young lady in the village yesterday. Think she'll be invited?''

Patty was at a loss as to how to respond to Auggie's question since she had no idea what young lady he'd seen. Marcus came to her rescue. ''I'm sure she will be, Auggie. An eligible bachelor draws a large attendance in this county.''

''Then all your parties must be well attended, Marcus, since you have three eligible bachelors in constant attendance.'' Charlie watched his friends in amusement as they took in his meaning.

''I am not...'' Marcus began, ''I mean—Augustus, perhaps, but—''

"The gentlemen in this county seem strangely averse to marriage, Sir Charles," Serena said in gently irony. "That is why your visit will create such a stir."

"I believe it is time my sister and I returned home," Daniel said, not caring for the turn of the conversation. "She is only just out of the sickroom, and I do not wish her to grow too tired."

As Serena rose, Sir Charles struggled to his feet in spite of her protest. "Nay, Miss Fenton, I could not miss the opportunity to bid you adieu." He drew her hand to his lips and then smiled at her. "I hope to be well enough to call on you in a few days' time. I have some lovely secrets to tell you about Daniel, which may be useful when he becomes too austere."

"I shall look forward to it, Sir Charles," Serena promised.

Lord Granville watched the leave-taking with irritation. Charlie was beginning to sound like the dandies in London, always mouthing insincerities. However, judging by the expression on Miss Fenton's face, he thought she rather liked his pretty words. Women!

"I shall withdraw also," Patty said.

Without hesitation, Sir Charles also kissed her hand. "I hope you have not worn yourself out offering me your hospitality, Miss Browne."

"Of course not, sir. You are a delightful guest."

"And your hospitality is only exceeded by your beauty," he murmured, his eyes twinkling.

Daniel, hearing this flattery, shook his head in disgust and dragged his sister from the room. Patty's rosy cheeks remained in his thoughts for the rest of the evening. He had not realized she was so susceptible to flirtation.

WITH SERENA RECOVERED from her illness and Sir Charles improving each day, Patty began preparations for their party. Much to her surprise, Marcus suggested she invite Miss Fenton to spend the day with her. He had several letters he needed written, and she could also help Patty address the invitations.

Nothing loath, Patty immediately sent a note to Serena the day after their dinner party, inviting her to come the following day.

"Another note from Granville House?" Daniel asked with some curiosity.

"Yes, Lord Granville requires several letters written tomorrow and Patty wondered if I might spend the day and assist her with invitations for the party."

"And will you accept?"

"Yes, of course. After all, I agreed to do what I could for Lord Granville, and I shall enjoy the entertainment as much or more than Sir Charles." She put the folded note beside her plate and continued her breakfast.

"I suppose they will invite every well-to-do family in the entire county," Daniel said with a sigh.

"That does not please you?"

"It is much ado about nothing," he said. "There are far better ways to spend my time."

"Perhaps if you are charming, you might find an increase in donations the next time you take up collections," Serena teased.

"True," Daniel returned with a grin, "or receive a generous stipend if a marriage takes place. Perhaps I should suggest to Marcus that he have more parties, to bring about more matches."

"I would not hold my breath waiting for marriages to take place. The atmosphere hereabouts does not appear to encourage Cupid to linger."

"You made a similar remark last evening. What precisely do you mean to say?" Daniel asked, watching his sister closely.

"As Sir Charles pointed out, there are three eligible bachelors in the immediate vicinity, but none seem inclined to marry."

Taking her words as a sign that she had more than a passing interest in matrimony, Daniel tried to probe delicately. "Do you have any particular bachelor in mind?"

"Yes, I do. You."

"I thought you might be interested in one of the eligible bachelors yourself," he protested, exasperated.

"Me? I told you I had no interest in marrying, Daniel. But *you* should marry—and the most obvious choice is Patty."

"Serena—"

"I think I have discovered the reason you have not offered for her," she continued, as if he had not spoken. "I believe it is because you feel your rank is too low in comparison to hers."

Daniel's face was flooded with colour and he studied his breakfast steadfastly, refusing to speak.

"I am correct, am I not? And if so, you have it as my opinion that you are being ridiculous."

"Serena, you know nothing about the ways of the world."

"Perhaps not, but I know that Patty's heart is breaking. Daniel, she loves you and no one else."

"There is a time and a place for all things, my dear," he said sternly. "You had best leave my future to me."

"But what if Sir Charles ... After all, he sees her every day."

"If she finds herself attracted to Charlie, then I wish her well. She must follow her heart."

"Surely you cannot wish her to do so?" Serena demanded.

Daniel pressed his lips firmly together before answering his sister. "She has attended the London Season twice without giving her heart to anyone."

"But, Daniel—"

"Serena, I have no choice. I cannot offer for Patty until I am sure she has exhausted all possible avenues for an appropriate marriage!" Daniel finally exclaimed, his patience at an end.

His sister immediately seized upon his words. "So if she does not succumb to Sir Charles's charm, you will offer for her?"

"I did not say that!" Daniel shoved back his chair and rose from the table, his appetite completely destroyed. "And if you should give Patty any hint of what has passed between us, I shall send you back to Mildred post-haste!"

Serena remained seated as her brother strode from the room. The pain in his eyes was hurtful to her. It was nonsensical for two people so much in love to continue in pain. Yet, she could not betray her brother's trust, even to help him.

Patty would never fall in love with Sir Charles when she already loved Daniel. But she might accept a proposal from him if she gave up hope of Daniel's ever offering.

Serena pondered the puzzle for some minutes before she discovered the solution. Of course: she must entice Sir Charles away from Patty. Patty would not mind, since she truly loved Daniel. She must be careful so as not to encourage Sir Charles to think that she wished for a proposal, of course, but she could flirt with him in a ladylike fashion and draw his attention away from Patty.

She wished she could confide in Patty, but she could not without explaining her reasons. With a sigh, she prepared her campaign, leaving the table to hurry into the parlour for paper and pen.

THE GENTLEMEN were already partaking of their second cup of tea when Patty joined them in the breakfast room. "Good morning. I apologize for my lateness."

"Your beauty is compensation enough, Miss Browne."

"Thank you, Sir Charles. It is a delight to have such a gentleman in our home," Patty responded with a smile.

Marcus frowned. He wanted Charlie to concentrate on Serena. He quickly changed the subject. "Lawrence left your letters at your place."

"Thank you, Marcus." She sat down as Lawrence prepared a plate for her and poured a cup of tea from the nearby pot. As she waited for her meal, she shuffled through the envelopes. "Oh, here is one from the vicarage. Was it delivered this morning, Lawrence?" she asked as the butler set her plate down before her.

"Yes, miss. The stable lad brought it a few minutes ago."

There was silence as Patty opened and read the note after seeking permission to do so from those at the table. "Oh."

"Is aught the matter?" Marcus demanded.

"No, not exactly. It is just that Serena proposes our escorting Sir Charles in a carriage ride about the area."

"That is an excellent idea, Charlie. Patty and Serena will make delightful guides."

"But I cannot go," Patty said. "My knitting class is this afternoon again. Serena must have forgotten. I am sorry, Sir Charles. Perhaps we may go another day."

"Tomorrow?" Marcus insisted.

"No, tomorrow we are writing the invitations for the party and Serena is helping you with your correspondence."

"It's not important," Sir Charles assured Patty. "I shall find much to occupy myself here."

Marcus was determined to instigate a way for Charlie to turn his attentions on Serena. "Why cannot Charlie and Miss Fenton ride out alone?"

"Marcus, that would not be proper," Patty assured him sternly. "You, who always preach propriety, should know that."

"Very well, Auggie shall accompany them."

Augustus, in the process of swallowing half a scone, choked. His brother had taken him completely unawares.

When he could speak, Auggie reminded Marcus that he was scheduled to oversee the planting in the north fields that day. "Love to, otherwise, of course," he assured Sir Charles with patent insincerity.

"Then I shall accompany them," Marcus announced. "There is nothing improper about that, I hope?" he added, looking at his sister.

"Not at all, brother," Patty assured him with raised brows.

"Really, Marcus, there is no need—"

"Yes, there is. Patty, please inform Miss Fenton of the change of plans and tell her we shall arrive at the vicarage at two of the clock."

"Good, that is precisely the time the knitting class begins. You may give me a ride to the vicarage."

CHAPTER ELEVEN

WHEN LORD GRANVILLE and his sister knocked on the door of the vicarage, they discovered Miss Fenton ready and waiting for the drive.

"I am sorry I cannot accompany you," Patty said, watching her friend with a frown. "You must have forgotten about the knitting class."

"Yes, I'm afraid I did, Patty. I am sorry, but I should be glad to show Sir Charles the area," Serena assured her.

Lord Granville, standing to one side, decided it was time he entered the conversation. "Since it would not be proper for you and Sir Charles to ride out alone, I have volunteered to act as your chaperon."

Serena's head snapped round in surprise. "I beg your pardon, my lord, I had not realized—that is, how kind of you to accompany us."

"It is my pleasure," he assured her, a grim smile on his face. In fact, it ought to have been a pleasure. Miss Fenton's glorious beauty was heightened by her blue wool gown and matching cloak. He only hoped

Charlie appreciated his sacrifice of an afternoon so that his friend could delight in Miss Fenton's beauty.

"Shall we be off?" he prompted.

Serena agreed and preceded him to the carriage. She wished to leave before Daniel could return and discover her duplicity.

Since Sir Charles had remained in the brougham to avoid exacerbating his injury, Serena was able to select the seat alongside him, leaving Lord Granville to sit with his back to the horses.

"I am so sorry Patty cannot join us," she said to Sir Charles, a charming smile on her face.

She was lying, Lord Granville realized, but for what purpose? Could she have a real tendre for Charlie? It would further his plans if such were the case.

For the next hour, Serena set out to charm Sir Charles, discussing the weather and the war on the Continent with equal aplomb. Both men were impressed with her knowledge. As Lord Granville had hoped, Sir Charles flirted with the young lady, though always keeping his remarks within the bounds of propriety.

Serena responded to the man beside her, but she was constantly aware of the frowning earl seated across from her. She felt he never took his eyes from her the entire afternoon. Perhaps he did want Sir Charles to offer for Patty.

Deciding to do a little probing herself, Serena introduced the subject of Patty and her generous efforts on Daniel's behalf. Sir Charles joined in her praise, assuring her that not only Patty's abilities, but also her beauty, had deeply impressed him.

Lord Granville interrupted his friend. "I'm sure Miss Fenton will do just as much as soon as she has adjusted to the move. After all, you have only recently joined your brother, haven't you, Miss Fenton?"

"Yes, but I shall never match Patty's talent for contributing so much to the parish."

"I am certain you will find other ways to assist your brother. Of course, I do not expect you to reside long at the vicarage."

Both Serena and Sir Charles looked askance at their host. "I am certain some lucky young man will marry you soon," he explained, directing a meaningful look at Sir Charles.

Charlie, glancing at the young lady beside him and then his friend, could only agree. He expected the earl to make an offer any day. Perhaps he should let his friend know that he approved of his choice. Taking Miss Fenton's hand, he carried it to his lips.

"*Whoever* that man shall be, he will be the luckiest man in the world to take you for his bride." Sir Charles sent a smile to Lord Granville, trying to convey to his friend that he approved his choice and wished to congratulate him upon it.

Marcus, interpreting his friend's erroneous conclusion, frowned and shook his head.

Both Sir Charles and Serena stared at him, and Marcus felt his cheeks grow warm with embarrassment. "I mean, of course, you are most right, Charlie. Perhaps Miss Fenton will meet her future husband at our party."

He avoided Serena's green-eyed gaze and turned the conversation to farming. Serena, excluded from the topic by lack of knowledge, considered the conversation just past. She did not believe her host really wanted Sir Charles to pursue his sister. Otherwise, he would have encouraged the man when he had praised Patty.

What confused her was his praise of herself. The very same thing had happened last night as well. That would indicate that the earl hoped Sir Charles would offer for her. But why would he concern himself with her matrimonial status—unless he wished to see her removed from the county? Melancholy stole over Serena as she realized the earl hoped to employ Sir Charles to remove an unwanted influence from his sister's life.

"Forgive us for boring you, Miss Fenton," Sir Charles said charmingly, drawing Serena back into the conversation. "When you were in London, did you ever chance across a Miss Mason?"

Serena noted a change in Sir Charles's demeanour, indicating how important the question was to him. "No, sir, I did not, but I did not move in the first circles of Society."

Lord Granville sat up straighter. "Is she connected in some way to General Mason?"

"Yes. She is his daughter," Sir Charles explained. "Did you not meet her?" He paused to consider as Lord Granville shook his head. "That is right. You left just before she and Mrs. Mason visited the general."

Neither Lord Granville nor Serena knew exactly how to phrase the question burning in both their breasts. Each wished to know just how close a friend Miss Mason was to Sir Charles, but they could not think how to broach the subject without prying into his privacy.

Sir Charles, unaware of the interest he'd created, said, "They visited the general many times the past two years, whenever we were not engaged in battle. I believe they returned to London in the intervals. It is too bad you did not meet her, Miss Fenton. I believe you would have liked each other."

"I'm sure we would have, sir," Serena said faintly.

"Unlike most ladies of the ton, she is well informed about the events on the Continent. As you are."

Serena thanked him for the compliment and then turned the conversation to more inconsequential matters. She was no longer required to feign a personal interest in Sir Charles, for his heart was already taken by a general's daughter. There was therefore no danger of his offering for Patty.

Lord Granville arrived at the same conclusion. He had wasted an afternoon providing Serena an opportunity to captivate his friend. Now what was he going to do about the beautiful young lady seated across from him? Auggie? No, his brother was not yet ready for marriage. Besides, he would need to marry someone with a large portion since Lord Granville intended to marry and have sons.

He could marry her himself, of course, his traitorous mind suggested, but that idea was immediately rejected. He required a conformable young lady, someone who would do his bidding without protest, someone who did not climb trees or wade in streams—which, of course, brought back the memory of Serena emerging from the water. His eyes fell to her covered bosom and his cheeks reddened when he discovered her watching him.

"Well, I believe we have seen all of interest in the vicinity," he said at once. "Shall we end our tour?"

His companions were in complete agreement with his suggestion.

"DID YOU ENJOY your ride with Sir Charles?" Patty asked the following morning when Serena joined her in the back parlour to address the invitations.

"The weather was fine," Serena said. "I hope it holds until after the party."

Patty noticed the deliberate change of subject but gave in gracefully to Serena's ploy. Her brother had seemed dejected last evening, but Sir Charles was as pleasant as ever.

Augustus opened the door to the parlour. "Patty, if Marcus should enquire, you haven't seen me."

"Auggie, what is the trouble?"

"I don't know. He is in a foul humour."

"But I thought the two of you were dealing very well together." Patty had been quite pleased with her brothers' agreeableness lately.

"Not today. I am ready to pack my bags for London."

"Surely you will remain until after the party, Mr. Browne," Serena said. "After all, that young lady you saw in the village would be disappointed if you did not."

Augustus was struck by her words. "I had forgotten about her."

"I'm sure whatever has upset Marcus will have been resolved in a day or two. Please be patient, Auggie," Patty pleaded.

"Very well. But I'm riding over to Lemming in any case," Augustus said, naming the small town beyond their village.

With Mr. Browne's departure, the ladies turned their attention back to the invitations for several minutes.

"Serena," Patty finally said hesitantly, "did anything occur yesterday to overset Marcus?"

"I did not notice anything, Patty. I promise I did not misbehave." Serena kept her gaze on her writing.

"Of course not! I did not mean to imply—that is, it is just that Marcus seemed unhappy last evening."

"Perhaps his wrist is troubling him."

"No, I don't think—"

Lawrence interrupted his mistress. "Miss Browne, a Mr. Peabody has called for Miss Fenton."

The two young ladies, stunned by Lawrence's announcement, stared at each other.

"What shall we do?" Patty whispered.

"I must receive him. He most likely has a message for me from Mildred. I do hope all is well."

"Very well, Lawrence. Show Mr. Peabody in."

The butler turned to do his mistress's bidding, but he did not like it. The man smelled of the shop and was not the kind of caller he was used to admitting to the big house.

When Mr. Peabody entered the back parlour, Patty knew at once why Serena had fled from her sister's home. Near fifty years of age, the man had a bulbous nose and a protruding stomach. His swagger was as ridiculous as were his clothes.

"Miss Fenton," he gushed, striding straight to her side to lift her hand to his thick lips.

Serena jerked her hand away before he could kiss it. "Permit me to present Miss Browne, the Earl of Granville's sister."

"My lady," the gentleman said, beaming. "It is my pleasure. I am so pleased Miss Fenton has found friends. I am sure she will wish to keep in touch with you."

Both ladies stared at him. Finally, Serena asked, "What do you mean, sir?"

"I carry a message to you from your sister, my dear. She has given her permission for our marriage. We shall be on our way as soon as you can make yourself ready."

"We shall do no such thing!" Serena returned heatedly. "My sister is not my guardian."

"I'm certain your brother will be in complete agreement when he realizes the advantages our marriage will provide you with."

"Mr. Peabody, I agree to go nowhere with you, nor will my brother approve of your proposal. You must leave at once."

His rampant geniality disappeared and Mr. Peabody's face took on a threatening expression. "You will do as you are told, Miss Fenton. After all, you are not of age. Your sister has your best interests at heart."

When he reached for her arm, Serena backed away from him, and Patty attempted to intervene. "Mr.

Peabody, I must ask that you leave at once. Miss Fenton—''

"Hello, Patty. I did not realize you had a guest," Marcus said, walking into the parlour. Lawrence, after due consideration, had decided to inform his master of the sort of visitor his sister was entertaining.

Relief washed over the two young ladies. Patty said, "Mr. Peabody, may I present my brother, the Earl of Granville."

"Mr. Peabody. Are you an acquaintance of Miss Fenton's?" Marcus asked, noting the angry snap of Serena's eyes.

"I am her fiancé, actually, come to return her to her sister's bosom."

"He is not my fiancé!" Serena protested, her eyes shooting sparks of fire.

"There seems to be some disagreement," Marcus said calmly.

"She is merely retiring," Mr. Peabody asserted in a hearty man-to-man tone intended to convince the earl of his familiarity with the lady in question.

"You have her brother's approval, of course?" Marcus asked, ignoring Serena's wrath.

"He will agree, rightly enough, when he knows how much I'm worth. She'll be well provided for."

Patty had placed a hand on Serena's arm, warning her not to interfere with her brother's handling of the situation. It was difficult to remain silent, but Serena did so.

"I take it you have never met Mr. Fenton."

Mr. Peabody chuckled. "Naw, but I know what these men of the church are: amiable but weak. And never with any blunt of their own. He'll be relieved to have her off his hands."

Looking down his nose, in bored tones, Marcus said, "Perhaps you are correct, sir, but I believe you should discuss your intent with Mr. Fenton before you depart."

"I'm planning to escort Miss Fenton back to the vicarage. I shall speak with Mr. Fenton before we return to London," the man assured the earl eagerly, seeing an opportunity to take Miss Fenton out of the house, away from this man's control. But he did not reckon on the earl's intelligence.

"Why do you not join us at the table for our noonday meal, Mr. Peabody? In the meantime, I'll locate the vicar."

"Don't want to put you to any trouble," Mr. Peabody protested, eyeing Serena as a hungry man does a feast.

She pressed against Patty in distaste and prayed the earl would not allow his desire to be rid of her to overcome his sense of fair play.

"Nonsense. I insist." Marcus stepped over to the bell-pull and Lawrence opened the door at once.

"Lawrence, please show Mr. Peabody to a chamber where he may refresh himself for luncheon."

The man reluctantly left the room, his eyes fixed on Serena until the door closed behind him. She slumped against Patty when he was gone.

Throwing her arms round her friend, Patty beamed at her brother. "I knew you would save her, Marcus."

Serena sat up, trying to gather her wits. "Yes, thank you, my lord. Though, of course, I could have—"

"Where is your brother?"

"He was to visit one of your tenants, Mr. Picket, today. He was injured several days ago, when a bull gored him, I believe."

"Yes. I'll send someone to Picket's and also to the vicarage. I do hope your brother will arrive before we are forced to dine with that man."

"I am sorry..."

"I assume you have no interest in Mr. Peabody?" the earl snapped, interrupting her.

Serena rose to her feet to stare coldly at her saviour. "No, my lord, I do not, nor have I ever led that...that man to suppose that I had the least interest in him."

"He appears to be quite wealthy."

If it were possible, Miss Serena Fenton's tone grew more icy. "My lord, I would rather starve than marry such a man."

Something in the earl responded with a silent cheer, but his face remained expressionless. "Very well, Miss Fenton. If you will retire to Patty's bedchamber until you are summoned, I shall locate your brother."

THE MESSAGE for the vicar reached him at the Picket cottage as he spoke with the injured man. Puzzled, he read the summons to Granville House. Excusing himself, he leapt into his tilbury and set a fast pace. Serena was with Patty this morning, and he could think of nothing which would require his presence.

When he was shown into the library where Marcus was awaiting him, he immediately demanded, "What is amiss? Is something wrong with Serena?"

"In a manner of speaking. A Mr. Peabody called here and insisted that your sister accompany him to London. He said he was her fiancé."

Mr. Peabody's description of churchmen came to Lord Granville's mind as he watched the anger build in the strong man across from him. It seemed that Mr. Peabody was in for a surprise.

"Where is he?" Daniel demanded, his voice laced with iron.

"I invited him to dine with us and directed Lawrence to show him to a bedchamber where he could refresh himself." He paused before asking, "Were you aware of his desire to marry your sister?"

"Yes. Serena told me of him . . . and of his behaviour."

Lord Granville stood. "His behaviour? He—"

"She said he did not harm her, but I believe he attempted to touch her."

"I should warn you that your sister Mildred has given her permission for the marriage to take place, and the man seems to think this gives him some justification."

"I shall certainly put him straight on that matter. If I might see him?"

Lord Granville moved to the bell-pull. "Shall I have him join us here, or do you wish to see him alone?" He hoped Mr. Fenton would allow him to be present. He had a growing desire to ensure Mr. Peabody received his just reward.

Daniel eyed his friend. What he saw must have pleased him, for he said, "Send for him here."

Satisfied, Marcus gave orders to Lawrence and joined Daniel before the fire to await the man's arrival.

Mr. Peabody entered the library with his hand extended, a genial smile upon his face. Lord Granville enjoyed the hesitation the man showed when Daniel stood, a tall, strong young man in his prime.

"Mr. Fenton, it is a pleasure to meet you," Mr. Peabody said.

When Daniel only stared at him, refusing to take his hand, the man let it drop to his side. "I suppose his lordship here has told you why I came." He reached inside his coat to pull out a letter. "Your sister Mildred sends you a message."

Daniel took the letter without a word and opened it. A brief scanning of the letter caused his lips to tighten in a fierce expression. His eyes flashed as he regarded Mr. Peabody.

"Sir, you are under a misapprehension if you think my sister has any control over Miss Fenton."

"Here now, son, you don't seem to understand the situation. I've got plenty of blunt—"

"You and your blunt, as you call it, had best return to London by the fastest means available. My sister shall not marry you. I intend her to marry a gentleman, and you do not fall into that category."

Red of face, Mr. Peabody advanced towards the vicar with his fists clenched. Lord Granville moved alongside his friend, a grim smile on his face, and the man halted.

"I care for your sister," the man insisted in a patently lascivious voice. "I'll take good care of her, better'n most. Ain't that something?"

"Sir, anyone who cared for a young lady would not force his intentions upon her as you have done," Daniel said stonily.

The man paled, his eyes shifting about. "I never— I don't know what she told you, but—"

"She told me enough to know that I should call you out. I refrained from doing so because I believed the incident concluded and you are a friend of my brother-in-law's.'' Daniel took a step closer. ''If you ever approach my sister again, however, I will not hesitate to do so. You and your blunt are not welcome, and I will explain that quite clearly in a letter to my sister.''

''You do that,'' the man snarled. ''I don't need to waste good blunt on a woman who ain't willing. There's plenty others better'n her. I ain't going to get taken in like Ned!''

Lord Granville stepped in front of a now raging Daniel. ''I believe you would be wise to leave now, Mr. Peabody, for I cannot be responsible for Mr. Fenton's reaction.''

Before Marcus had finished his speech, Mr. Peabody was moving towards the door, having read his mistake in Daniel's eyes. Without waiting for an escort, he hurried from the house.

Once the door had closed, Marcus turned to face his still-furious friend. ''You know, Daniel, for a man of the cloth, you could become quite violent.''

''That is called righteous anger, Marcus, and utterly justified in this instance.''

CHAPTER TWELVE

WHEN THE TWO YOUNG LADIES were summoned to lunch, they were greatly relieved to discover Mr. Fenton in the place of Mr. Peabody. Though they each asked several questions, both Mr. Fenton and Lord Granville simply said Mr. Peabody had accepted his refusal and chosen to return to London.

Serena shuddered at the thought of the man. She raised her eyes to find Lord Granville's gaze fixed on her. She squared her shoulders before saying, "Thank you for your assistance, my lord. I must apologize for bringing my difficulties to your door."

With her vibrant green eyes and wisps of auburn hair framing her creamy face, Serena was enchanting in Marcus's eyes. It was with difficulty that he turned from her, murmuring, "I did but little."

Feeling snubbed, Serena was silent for the remainder of the meal. Daniel, having observed the exchange between his sister and his friend, attempted to carry the conversation. Since Sir Charles was his only assistant in his endeavour, they were both to find it a laborious task.

When the meal was completed, Serena stiffly enquired of Lord Granville if she were still needed to assist him with his correspondence.

"Thank you, Miss Fenton, but I'm sure you would be better advised to return home to recuperate from your difficult morning. Patty will assist me."

Patty regarded her brother in surprise but said nothing. Daniel, however, realized Marcus was making a deliberate attempt to avoid his sister. It appeared that his efforts as Cupid were a complete failure. With thanks to Lord Granville for his assistance, Daniel led Serena to the door.

He looked back over his shoulder to discover Patty and Charlie in close conversation. His heart lurched in anguish. The jealousy he'd hoped to stir in Marcus's breast filled his instead.

HAVING ABSENTED HIMSELF the day before, Augustus missed the excitement of Mr. Peabody's visit. It did not appear to him that his brother's humour had improved when they met at the breakfast table the following morning. He took his place with a full plate and kept his attention trained on it.

Patty joined her brothers before Sir Charles had descended. She, too, was melancholy, since Daniel's behaviour had continued to be discouraging. It seemed to her that since their return from London, everything had gone amok.

The morning post was brought in by Lawrence just as Sir Charles entered the breakfast room. The fact that Augustus received a letter was not noted by anyone until he choked on his tea.

"Auggie, are you quite all right?" Patty asked, rising in alarm.

He waved her back to her seat. "Fine, er, fine. Just swallowed too quickly."

Lord Granville, watching his brother closely, asked, "Bad news in the post?"

Auggie quickly folded the letter and shoved it into his pocket. "No, no, just a note from a friend."

He reapplied himself to his breakfast, keeping his gaze lowered. Gradually, conversation was resumed and shortly thereafter, Augustus excused himself.

Patty eyed the almost full plate left by her brother and knew that something was amiss. If there was one thing to be counted upon, it was surely Augustus's healthy appetite. After breakfast, she searched for him but he was nowhere to be found.

She decided to call on Serena, but was halted in the entry hall by Sir Charles.

"Miss Browne, I have a great favour to ask of you."

"Why, of course, Sir Charles."

"I wonder if you made the acquaintance of a Miss Mason while you were in London?"

"Miss Mason? Why, yes, I believe I did. She was only present for part of this past Season, but I spoke with her several times." Patty recalled a serious young lady, well-informed on the events occurring across the Channel.

"Ah, yes, how nice for you both. I wondered . . . you see—" Sir Charles paused, his cheeks red, much to Patty's surprise "—that is, I wondered if it might be possible to invite Miss Mason and her mother to our party."

Comprehension dawned on Patty. "We would be delighted to invite Miss Mason and Mrs. Mason. I gather, then, that I should not bruit it about that we have *four* eligible bachelors at our party."

Sir Charles beamed in relief. "You are absolutely correct, Miss Browne. Thank you so much for your understanding."

"I am delighted I could be of service, Sir Charles."

"I would have asked earlier, but I thought Miss Mason was still on the Continent. I received word in the post this morning that she is back in London."

"We shall be delighted to have them both as our guests as long as they would care to stay."

"I say, Miss Browne, that is deuced generous of you."

"Not at all, sir. I shall enjoy renewing my acquaintance with Miss Mason." Patty curtsied and took her leave of her brother's friend.

She could not wait to inform Serena of this newest event. At least *someone* wanted to marry. She wished her brother would consider marriage to Serena, but after observing his dismissive behaviour of yesterday, she had all but given up on that account. Perhaps their family was doomed to die out, unless Augustus found someone to marry.

"YOU KNEW?" Patty demanded when Serena evinced no surprise at the news.

"No, not precisely, but something in his voice gave his feelings away when Sir Charles asked me if I'd met Miss Mason." She paused before saying, "In truth, Patty, I think that is what has upset your brother."

"Why should Sir Charles's attachment disturb Marcus?"

Serena ducked her head, afraid of showing her emotions. "I believe your brother hoped Sir Charles would offer for me and thereby remove me from the vicinity."

"But why—"

"I believe him to be concerned that I may lead you astray, as I did when we went wading on the picnic."

The strong possibility of Serena's being correct in her surmise could not be denied. Patty reached out and clasped her friend's hand. "I'm sorry, Serena. I tried to explain to Marcus—"

"Do not trouble yourself. Perhaps we shall grow old together, in spite of your brother's desires."

"If it is to be so, I shall derive great enjoyment from your friendship, as I already have," Patty said softly, clasping Serena's hand. They smiled at each other in understanding.

"Patty? Your pardon, Miss Fenton, but I must speak to my sister," Augustus said as he pushed in front of Mrs. Washburn.

"Well, I never," the housekeeper protested. "I tried to announce him, Miss Fenton."

"It's quite all right, Mrs. Washburn." The housekeeper left the room and Serena rose. "I'll leave you two alone."

She retreated to her brother's study, wondering what could have upset Mr. Browne so. After only a few minutes, Patty, along with Mr. Browne, entered the study.

"Serena, I know we should not involve you in our difficulties,but—"

"Your family rescued me from Mr. Peabody. If I can be of assistance, I shall be glad of the opportunity to return the favour."

Augustus said nothing, looking to his sister for assistance. Patty took his hand and they both seated themselves on the sofa.

"It is just this. Auggie agreed to buy a horse from a...a friend. Then, he incurred some gambling debts which made it impossible for him to pay for the horse. So he came here and wrote his friend a note, advising him that they would close their agreement when he returned to London." With an apologetic glance at her brother, she added, "Auggie thought he would wait here until the next quarter began and he received his allowance."

"Wasn't such a bad plan," Augustus mumbled. "Would've worked except that Tollersham needs the blunt."

"Has he written you?"

"He's here, at the Eagle's Claw Inn in Lemming, and wants Auggie to meet him there to conclude their business. He's brought the horse in question with him."

"Oh, dear." Serena could see the difficulty. "What shall you do?"

"That is the difficulty. We do not know what to do. I had hoped you might be able to suggest something for you are much more quick-witted than I. Have you any ideas?"

Serena shook her head at her friend. "I assume it is quite impossible to speak to the earl?"

"He won't give me any advances. He told me so," Augustus said glumly. "And I would rather he not know of this. We've got on so well of late."

The two young ladies nodded in understanding. "Surely we can devise some plan to rescue you," Serena said firmly, and the three young people put their heads together to find a way out of Augustus's difficulty.

"SERENA, I am so afraid our plan will not be successful," Patty muttered, a frown on her face, the following day. She was riding beside her friend in her brother's brougham, dressed as a ladies' maid.

"I know. But since none of us have enough money to pay for the horse and Mr. Browne will not go to his brother, it is our only hope."

Patty frowned even more. "It is not that Marcus would not help Augustus. It is just—"

"I understand, Patty," Serena assured her. "I have witnessed your brother's concern and care for you both. But I daresay were I in Augustus's predicament, I would not apply to Daniel for assistance. Sometimes their help is harder to bear than their anger."

"Yes, that is it, exactly. I just did not wish you to think badly of Marcus."

"Your brother is a fine man, even if he is a trifle strait-laced." With a shudder, she added, "Let us hope he never gets wind of our activities today, or he might compel Daniel to send me back to London."

"But it is Auggie who is at fault, and me for involving you."

"Never mind. We shall keep our scheme a secret. Is my bonnet on straight?" she asked.

"Yes. You look most elegant."

"I ought to, since you borrowed the Granville diamonds to lend me an air of wealth," Serena said, grinning at her friend. "*That* is what may destroy us if we do not return them at once."

"Oh, look, there is Augustus with someone. It must be Mr. Tollersham."

Serena assessed the two men at length as the carriage drew near. Mr. Tollersham appeared a dandy, with his shirtpoints absurdly high. Her gaze moved on to the horses standing near the two men.

"Dear Heaven!" she muttered.

"What is the matter?"

"Look at that bag of bones. Surely that cannot be the horse Mr. Browne agreed to purchase? Why, anyone could see—" She broke off, afraid that she would offend Patty.

"I know," Patty agreed with a sigh. "Marcus says that Auggie has an abominable eye for horse flesh." She stared at the animal Serena pointed out. "Now I do not feel so badly about duping Mr. Tollersham. But your part will be more difficult."

"Daniel says greed makes men blind. Let us hope that he is right." Serena composed herself and as the carriage passed the two men, she called to the driver, one specially selected by Patty to hold his tongue. "Jacob, stop the carriage at once!"

The two men looked up in surprise. At least, Mr. Tollersham evinced surprise. Augustus radiated relief but the ladies hoped his companion did not notice.

"My good man," Serena called imperiously, beckoning the gentlemen to approach the carriage. "Whose animal is that?" She pointed to the bay standing with the other two horses. The white markings on its face gave her the perfect ploy.

Augustus stepped forward, as planned. "Do you mean the bay, madam?"

"Yes, of course I mean the bay. What other horse could I possibly mean?"

Since three horses were tethered to the limb of a tree, Mr. Tollersham appeared confused. Augustus, privy to the script, however, replied, "I am the owner of the bay, madam."

"Good. How much will you sell him to me for? He is the perfect match to a horse I already own. Their resemblance is uncanny." She stared at Augustus. "He is not stolen, is he?"

"No, of course not. I would never deal—"

"Very well. I'll offer a thousand crowns."

Since Augustus had revealed he'd agreed to pay three hundred crowns, Serena expected the inflated offer to excite Mr. Tollersham's interest.

"A thousand— Here now, Auggie, that horse belongs to me."

Augustus turned to his friend. "What are you about, Tolly? We are meeting here for me to pay you for the horse. We agreed upon a price."

Mr. Tollersham, his eyes avidly scanning the young woman's appearance, mentally tallying up the value of her jewels and her carriage, turned back to his friend, drawing him away from the equipage.

"We discussed the price, but since you have not paid me the money, the horse is still mine."

"But, Tolly—"

"There will be no discussion, Auggie. I shall have another horse to sell you next month, but this horse matches the lady's other animal. You would not deny her a matched pair, would you?"

"I ain't promising to buy another horse, Tolly. If you won't sell me this one, then you can look elsewhere for your next mark."

"Of course, of course," Tolly agreed, turning back to the carriage before Augustus had finished speaking.

"Well, young man?" said Serena, addressing Augustus. "Are you or are you not the owner of that horse?"

"I am the owner, madam," said Tollersham. "My transaction with the gentleman there has not been completed, and until money has changed hands, I retain ownership."

Augustus stood to one side, having temporarily forgotten his role. Serena looked at him sharply. "Then be about your business, sir. I deal only with the rightful owner."

Recalled to his role, Augustus nodded in their direction, trying to hide his grin, mounted his horse and rode down the road towards the vicarage.

"My lady, I don't think..." Patty murmured, speaking for the first time and placing a hand on Serena's arm.

"Nonsense, Sukie! Papa said I could have whatever I wished for my birthday. If I choose this animal, he shall be pleased."

Mr. Tollersham almost licked his lips when he heard his buyer addressed by a title. He opened the carriage door and assisted Serena as she descended. "I'm sure your father will admire your taste, my lady. This animal is a fine specimen. In fact, I'm not sure I can sell him to you for one thousand crowns."

Without replying, Serena walked slowly around the animal. Mr. Tollersham accompanied her, interjecting praise into the silence.

When Serena turned back towards the carriage, he asked, "Where shall I send the steed, my lady?"

"I have changed my mind. He is not as I thought him to be."

"Changed...changed your mind? But you cannot. You offered a thousand crowns. You are obliged to honour your offer." His growing anger hastened Serena's step.

As she reached the carriage, he grasped her arm, pulling her to a stop.

"Sir, unhand me."

The driver and the footman both stepped down from their positions and Mr. Tollersham did as he was bade. Both men had been chosen for their size as well as their discretion.

"My lady, we made an agreement. Gentlemen do not go back on their word."

Serena was assisted into the carriage by the footman. After seating herself, she looked down at the man. "Sir, in the event that you have not noticed, *I* am not a gentleman. Even if I were, however, *you* are the one who said an agreement was not final until money changed hands. I am only following your rules. I have changed my mind and I do not wish to purchase your horse for any amount."

"But—but—"

"Drive on, Jacob," Serena ordered regally, sinking back into the squabs and staring straight ahead.

The two young ladies maintained their poses quietly, but their faces were beaming with their success. Half a mile away, Patty peeked over her shoulder to be certain Mr. Tollersham was not following them. When she ascertained that he was nowhere in sight, she grabbed Serena's hand.

"We did it! Oh, Serena, you were perfect! You were more starched up than the richest dowager in the land!"

Though she was grinning, as well, Serena said, "Mind your tongue, young lady. I was elegant, not starched up!" She lifted her nose in the air and struck a snobbish pose often seen among certain members of the ton.

"I am so grateful, Serena, as Auggie will certainly be. If you had not engineered this plan, I do not know what we would have done." Patty hugged her friend. "At least one thing has gone aright."

"Others may follow, dear Patty. You must be patient."

Essaying a weak smile, Patty nodded. "Of course. I must not wallow in self-pity when you have so beautifully solved our difficulty."

Serena reached up to undo the diamond brooch which was fastened at the neck of her green wool gown. "I must return these to you at once."

"Oh, do not take them off here. I might misplace them. When we reach our rendezvous, I shall put them all at once in the leather pouch." She pointed up ahead. "There is the clump of trees where Augustus promised to await us."

"I hope he didn't forget the place," Serena murmured drily.

Patty giggled. "He almost forgot to leave, didn't he? But he played his part very well, don't you agree?"

"Yes, he did, but I do think he should not deal again with Mr. Tollersham. The man is not to be trusted."

"I agree. I shall try to persuade him."

Jacob swung the carriage off the road and pulled it into a copse. Patty saw a horseman just ahead. "There he is, Jacob."

Augustus, however, was not alone. Just behind him was Lord Granville, a grim expression on his face.

CHAPTER THIRTEEN

JACOB, for all his size, turned pale. He knew when he could expect to incur his master's wrath. No one moved, the two young women staring at the big man sitting his horse like a stone.

Augustus was the first to speak. "Marcus, I promise you, the ladies had nothing to do with . . . with anything."

"Then perhaps you will explain why Miss Fenton is wearing the Granville jewels," Marcus asked silkily.

There was a dreadful moment of silence. Serena itched to snatch the jewels in question from her body and throw them out of the carriage, but she wisely refrained.

Perhaps it was the footman's uncomfortable cough, but Marcus remembered the servants and abruptly ordered Jacob to drive to the vicarage. The man obeyed his master at once, swinging the carriage back onto the road.

Serena and Patty were aware that the two horsemen had fallen in behind the carriage, but they did not turn around.

"What do you suppose he'll do?" Serena whispered to Patty.

"I don't know. I am afraid to find out."

Serena knew exactly how her friend felt. She only hoped Daniel was not at home. She had had great intentions about considering the repercussions before taking action ever again. But she could not refuse to help when her friends were in difficulty. After all, Lord Granville had assisted her when Mr. Peabody had threatened her. Now he would probably send her to Mr. Peabody with his blessing.

When the carriage halted in front of the vicarage, the two young ladies waited to be handed down, just as well-brought-up young ladies did, but neither of them imagined such deportment would appease Lord Granville in the least.

Much to Patty and Serena's dismay, Mrs. Washburn assured the earl that the vicar was indeed at home.

"He would be," Patty muttered, but said nothing else as Marcus frowned at her.

"We shall announce ourselves, Mrs. Washburn. He is in the study?"

"Yes, my lord. I'll bring a tea tray."

"Thank you. And if you will offer the same to the servants, I believe they are in need of sustenance."

"Why, o'course, my lord. Right away."

Lord Granville herded his little troop down the hall to the study and rapped smartly upon the door before opening it.

"Daniel? May we come in?"

"Of course, Marcus," Daniel said, rising as his friend opened the door wider. "Why, I did not realize there were so many of you," he said lightly, until his eyes lit upon the diamonds gracing his sister's person. A frown deepened on his brow and he stepped to his sister's side. "Serena, what is the meaning of this?"

"I would also like the answer to that question," Lord Granville said harshly. "So far I have received no reply."

Serena stared at the book-lined wall. She did not wish to disappoint Daniel again for all the world. "Daniel, I—" she began and then stopped. Struck by an inspiration, she began once more. "You see, I only wanted to view the famous Granville jewels, and when Patty was kind enough to show them to me, she very generously suggested I might try them on. I know it was foolish of me, Daniel, but I thought it would cause no harm if I wore them while we went for a brief drive." She looked up appealingly. "You know how I have always enjoyed play-acting."

Daniel pushed back a lock of auburn hair which had loosed from beneath her bonnet. "Yes," he agreed with a sigh, "you always did enjoy pretending."

"And apparently still does, if that is to be her explanation."

All eyes swung towards Marcus.

"Daniel, Augustus was lurking in that copse down the road, waiting for the ladies. Patty is dressed as a lady's maid. Do you really suppose this elaborate scheme is merely a matter of play-acting, so that Serena may pretend to be Lady Granville and wear the family jewels?"

His scorn angered Serena, and as was her habit when her ire was provoked, she spoke without regard to the consequences. "You are quite right, my lord. I would never go to such lengths to pretend to be Lady Granville. It is not a position to which I aspire!"

"That is well and good, young lady, because your conduct places that position beyond your reach!"

Glaring at each other, they did not hear Daniel's call to order until he moved between them.

"Please, Marcus, Serena, can we not discuss this calmly? I fear all this anger will do little to clarify matters."

"This is all my fault," Augustus confessed abruptly.

"No, no, Auggie, it is mine," Patty claimed.

"You are both in error. It is mine, and since your brother has always condemned my behaviour, it will make no difference if he does so once more." Serena stared belligerently at her adversary.

Mrs. Washburn's arrival with the tea tray gave Daniel an opportunity to damp down tempers, and he insisted they all be seated and take a cup of tea before any more words were spoken. He requested that Patty pour out since he feared that Serena might chuck a teacup at Lord Granville if she were presented with an empty one.

Before accepting her tea, Serena carefully removed the ear-drops, large cluster pin and several bracelets. Since Patty was occupied with pouring tea, she leant towards Mr. Browne. "Sir, do you have the leather pouch for the jewels?"

Patty set down the silver teapot. "No, Serena. It is in my reticule." She took that item out of her bag and received the jewels from Serena.

"You are responsible for giving Miss Fenton the family jewels?" Marcus demanded sternly.

"I am responsible for urging Serena to use them while she was assisting us out of our difficulty," Patty replied, facing her brother squarely. "She neither asked for nor wanted the opportunity of wearing them."

"I have not yet received my tea, Patty." Daniel's gentle reminder brought a blush to Patty's cheeks, and she returned to her duties.

Lord Granville sipped his tea and waited for Daniel, as his host, to resume the conversation.

Daniel took a sip of the hot liquid before setting it down and saying, "I gather Mr. and Miss Browne have...had a problem which has now been resolved." All three involved nodded their heads, several of them watching Lord Granville warily out of the corner of their eyes.

Turning to his friend, Daniel said, "Marcus, I would not normally intervene in personal matters concerning your family, but since Serena is involved..."

Lord Granville nodded. "Proceed, Daniel. I am anxious to hear the explanation."

Patty and Serena exchanged guarded looks, but Augustus cleared his throat. "'Tis my fault, not the girls'. I, er, owed someone and couldn't pay." He hung his head, shamefaced.

Frowning, Lord Granville said, "A gentleman always pays his debts, Auggie."

His brother only nodded, saying nothing.

Serena, however, could not remain silent. "There is no question Mr. Browne is a gentleman, my lord. But the other man involved was a swindler, charging an exorbitant sum for a horse which was no more than a bag of bones."

Mr. Browne kept his head down and Lord Granville groaned. He could easily believe Miss Fenton's disclaimer. His brother was a notoriously bad judge of horseflesh and an easy mark for every trickster in London.

In a deceptively gentle voice, Daniel asked, "How would you know to what manner of man Mr.

Browne owed money? Or what the horse in question looked like?"

"I . . ." Serena began. Stopping, she sent a silent plea to her brother. "I know I should not have agreed to the scheme, Daniel, but they are my friends. And Lord Granville did not hesitate to protect me when Mr. Peabody wished to take me to London."

"Of course I did not!" Marcus exclaimed, a frown on his face. "A gentleman would never abandon a lady in distress."

With a stubborn lift of her chin, Serena replied, "A lady would never abandon friends in distress."

For the first time, Lord Granville's lips curved upwards. "*Touché*, Miss Fenton."

Daniel, still not satisfied, asked, "In what manner did you 'assist' your friends?"

"Daniel, it is truly my fault Serena became involved. I insisted we consult her because I could think of no answer to our problem."

Turning to look at the young lady seated behind the teapot, the vicar asked quietly, "And you did not feel you could confide in me?"

"Daniel!" Patty sank her teeth into her bottom lip. "I . . . you . . . I knew you would advise us to apply to Marcus, and I did not wish to place Auggie in an awkward position."

"Am I so ferocious when crossed?"

"Yes!" Three voices answered Lord Granville in unison.

Surprised, Lord Granville thought back over the past two years. "Perhaps I have been, er, rather strict with you, Auggie, but I only wanted to ensure that our sudden wealth and rank did not adversely influence you."

"But—" Augustus began before a wry look crossed his face. "I would rather not agree, Marcus. However, I daresay if I had had more money and freedom, Tollersham probably would have fleeced me for even more."

"Tollersham?" Marcus snapped. "He's an ugly customer. You allowed the ladies to deal with him?"

"We came to no harm," Serena hastily assured him.

"He did not touch you?"

Serena regretted her honest nature. "He—he only took hold of my arm."

"Why didn't you stop him, Augustus?" Marcus demanded sternly, fire in his eyes.

"He had already departed. It was part of our plan," Serena again replied.

"Augustus?" Lord Granville only said.

"Patty and Serena said it was the only way the ruse would work." Augustus squared his shoulders and looked his brother in the eye. "However, you are right. I should never have left them there alone with such a disreputable character."

Nodding in satisfaction, Marcus turned his attention upon the two young ladies. "I think it is time we heard about this marvellous plan of yours."

Serena looked at Patty and then said, "Daniel always says greed blinds people."

She was relieved to see a twinkle in Daniel's eyes as he murmured, "I am glad someone listens to my sermons."

"And?" Marcus prodded, his eyes never leaving Serena.

"We decided that if Mr. Tollersham cried off from their agreement, then Mr. Browne would not owe him any money at all, and he would not have dishonoured his name."

When she paused, Marcus asked, "Yes, but how did you accomplish this, or did you?"

"It was a wonder, Marcus," Augustus broke in, laughter in his voice. "I've never seen Tolly's eyes grow so large. When Miss Fenton offered a thousand crowns for that dreadful horse, he couldn't back out of our agreement fast enough."

Now it was Daniel's turn to demand information. "Serena! You offered a thousand crowns for a horse? You do not have that kind of—"

"Of course not, Daniel. But Mr. Tollersham explained that it was his opinion there was no agreement until money had changed hands. Therefore, when he insisted we had one, I explained that as I had not paid him any money, any agreement was null and void."

"And the jewels you wore along with Patty dressed as a lady's maid were to assure him you were able to afford such a price?" Marcus guessed.

"Yes, and I addressed her as 'my lady,' just to convince him."

Serena, her eyes on her brother, hurriedly added, "I know it was dishonest, Daniel, but, truly, the man was a thief, stealing Mr. Browne's money, to expect him to purchase that horse for any price."

Daniel cleared his throat. "I understand your reasoning, my dear, but I cannot be comfortable with such deliberate deceit."

Marcus, the corners of his lips quivering, attempted to sound stern. "Daniel is quite right. While I detest the man, I'm not sure deceiving him was proper. I intend to deal with him, however. And in future, Augustus, I suggest you bring your problems to me, not to your sister. And I shall attempt to increase my tolerance."

"Yes, brother. And I'm learning a great deal about horseflesh this winter. Perhaps I won't be such a flat when next I'm in London."

Marcus cuffed his brother on the shoulder. "I should hope not. But you have been of real assistance to me, Auggie. I am glad we are dealing better with each other."

Augustus grinned at his brother in acknowledgement of the compliment before saying, "If I might be excused, I did promise Murchison I would accompany him on a visit to one of our tenants regarding repairing his fence.'' With a nod to the men and a whispered thank-you to his sister and her friend, Augustus left the room.

"You have done well, Marcus," Daniel commented quietly.

"Not alone, I haven't. I have been too harsh at times. Thanks to you and Patty, and even Miss Fenton, things have turned out very well."

"Me?" Serena asked in surprise.

Marcus smiled as his eyes dwelt on her beauty. "Yes, Miss Fenton. In spite of my early condemnation of your manners, I have discovered you to be a good influence on all my family."

"Including yourself, Lord Granville?" she asked.

"Even me, my dear Miss Fenton. I will allow that I have fought against your influence, but your *joie de vivre* has added a spark of life which I had all but lost over the past two years."

"Then you are not angry about what took place today?"

Raising his eyebrows, Lord Granville murmured, "I am not angry, but I would not want you to believe that I would encourage such behaviour again. You might have been injured."

."But we were not."

"You were not as sanguine when Mr. Peabody came to call."

Serena pouted, an action that, in Lord Granville's opinion, made her rosebud mouth appear fuller and more enticing. "That is not fair. I am quite confident I would have found a solution, had you not come to my rescue."

Daniel and Patty, sitting as observers, exchanged a speaking look.

"Yes, and it is that imagination which so often leads you astray. That is why I had hoped Charlie would offer for you and take you away before any real disaster occurred."

Though he only confirmed her earlier belief, Serena was stung by his words. "Do not despair, my lord. I have no intention of concerning myself with you and yours ever again."

CHAPTER FOURTEEN

DANIEL CLEARED his throat. "That will prove to be rather awkward, my dear."

His audience stared at him. He cleared his throat once more. "I promised myself I would wait until after Patty's third Season before I approached you, again, Marcus, but—"

"Again?" Patty shrieked, turning a ferocious glare on her brother.

Startled, Marcus echoed her sentiments. "Again? When did you ever—"

"I did not," Daniel hastily corrected. Patty turned back to him, her gaze demanding an explanation. "Though I had never met you, my love, I already knew a great deal about you from the letters you wrote to Marcus when we were together at school. When I finally met you after Marcus's rise in rank and you were... you were all and more than I had ever dreamed possible."

"Oh, Daniel," Patty whispered, her heart in her eyes.

"You seemed to return my regard, so I thought to ask Marcus for your hand. But before I could find the appropriate words, he told me of his plan to take you to London and find you a husband worthy of your rank."

"That was why you..." Marcus began and then trailed off as he thought back to that interview.

"And you allowed that to stop you?" Patty asked, her voice quavering.

"No, my dearest heart," Daniel assured her, crossing the room to go down on one knee and carry her hand to his lips. "I merely promised myself I would stand aside and allow you the choice. If you preferred titles and fortune, then I would always be your friend... and I would always love you."

Miss Cleopatra Browne showed no appreciation for his sentiments. Jumping to her feet, she shoved him away, knocking him to the floor. "If *I* chose? If *I* chose, Daniel Fenton? What choice did you give me? You refused to even hint of your feelings! Do you know how I suffered? How near I was to despair?"

Mr. Fenton appeared stunned by the raging tigress towering over him. In the flicker of an eyelash, however, the tigress dissolved into a weeping kitten as she subsided in her chair, tears rushing down her cheeks.

"For what it's worth, Daniel," Marcus said over his sister's sobs, "you have my blessing."

Daniel, anxious to console his love, nodded his thanks.

Before the vicar could turn his attention back to the love of his life, Marcus added, "I shall escort your sister to the parlour so you may conduct your proposal in private." Daniel nodded again, eager to be alone with Patty.

Marcus, however, was not finished with the conversation. "I assume you will return the favour?"

His words caught even Patty's attention. "Marcus," she demanded, sniffing, "whatever do you mean?"

Lord Granville smiled at Serena. "I have decided I ought to marry Miss Fenton. She requires a strong hand on the ribbons, and I appear to be the only one eligible for that position."

Serena's glare could not be construed as loverlike by the most optimistic suitor, but it did not daunt Lord Granville. "Shall we allow Daniel and Patty some privacy, Serena?"

She rose and swept past him as if he did not exist. "I shall retire to my chamber."

Marcus swiftly followed her into the hall and caught her arm as he pulled the door to behind him. "Surely you will not abandon me to my own company, my dear?"

"Release me, my lord. I'll not stand for your making sport of me."

Lord Granville stared down into her green eyes, angry sparks radiating from them. "Of course not, my love."

"I am not your love!" Serena protested, even as her limbs weakened.

He led her into the parlour and closed the door behind the two of them. "But I must be truthful, Serena. You *are* my love. I shall admit that I did everything in my power to resist your charms, but I found it impossible."

"I have seen no evidence of your submission," she assured him, her chin raised.

"Ah, submission. I do not believe I spoke of *my* submission," Marcus said with a grin. "A wife should submit herself to her husband, my love, not the other way round."

"Then it is a good thing we are not husband and wife, my lord."

He pulled her against him, wrapping his arms about her. "We shall work out an agreement, dearest Serena, for I find I cannot live without you at my side."

"You must not offer marriage unless...unless you love me truly," Serena declared, but her voice trailed to a whisper, her gaze fixed upon his face.

"I must offer you marriage, my love, because I *do* love you truly."

"I will not be ignored, as Mildred's husband ignores her."

"Ignoring you would be impossible, my dear," Lord Granville assured the young lady before him.

"I—I sometimes act before I think, Marcus."

"I have noticed."

"I am not always properly behaved."

"True."

"I do not like to be ordered about."

"Duly noted. Now will you agree to marry me?"

She stared up at him, her hands clutching his lapels. "Even knowing these things, you would still marry me?"

"I find I cannot help myself, my love. You are in my thoughts constantly. I cannot sleep for want of you."

Her cheeks turned a fiery red. "There . . . there is one more difficulty, Marcus."

"What is that, Serena?" he asked, a smile playing about his lips.

"Mr. Peabody kissed me once," she explained, peeping up at him to witness the anger flash in his eyes.

"I ought to have challenged the man!"

"No, it is just . . . I did not like it."

"I promise you that I am more skilful than Mr. Peabody. Shall we see if my kisses disgust you? If so, you have only to tell me and I shall go away."

Serena considered his offer before lifting her lips trustingly to his.

"Well?" he asked a moment later, his voice rough with emotion.

"I think we must practise more," Serena murmured dreamily, a smile on her rosy lips.

THERE WAS AN awkward silence after the door closed, each occupant of the room avoiding the others' gaze. Then, as if planned, they both spoke.

"Patty—"

"Why—"

Daniel, after both came to a confused stop, continued, "Please, Patty, what were you about to ask?"

She stood and walked across the room, her back to him. "You said you had promised yourself to wait three Seasons. Why have you spoken now?"

"Because I am weak," he muttered. "I thought I could be patient, but I saw our friendship... us...growing further and further apart. Today, when you revealed that you took your worries to Serena, rather than to me, I could not bear it another minute." He strode over to grasp her shoulders and turn her to face him. "Patty, *I* want to be your confidant, your friend, your... lover."

Tears welled in her eyes. "Daniel, I want those things, also. But I was so discouraged. I began to imagine you did not—that you had decided I was not an appropriate wife for a vicar."

He pulled her to him, wrapping his arms tightly around her. "You are more than I could ever hope for in a wife, my love. Your skills, your concern, your tenderness, your beauty—"

"Oh, Daniel, I am not a beauty," she protested as she blinked away her tears.

Tilting up her chin, he stared into her blue eyes. "Cleopatra Browne, you rival your namesake for beauty, only yours is of a greater depth, a greater wealth, because you are beautiful both inside and out."

She nestled her head under his chin and clung to him. "I love you, Daniel. I am so glad you spoke today." She lifted her head again. "You see, I promised Marcus I would accept another's proposal if you did not ask for my hand before the Season began."

"What? Why would he—"

"He feared I was pursuing you against your wishes."

"He could not be so foolish!"

Patty's eyebrows rose. "Really, Daniel, you gave no indication. If you had, I would not have been so distraught."

"Distraught? I thought you a trifle forward at times, but not distraught," Daniel said, teasing, his eyes sparkling with mirth as he watched Patty's cheeks flush.

"At least I knew my heart's desire. As you did when you decided to play Cupid for your sister and my brother."

It was Daniel's turn to blush. "I should not have—"

"Are you not happy that they are to be married?"

"Of course I am extremely pleased, but a proper vicar should not be tempted to play such a role."

Patty reached up to smooth away the frown on his brow. "Who better to help people find true love than a man of the cloth? After all, the Bible tells us that love is the greatest of all things."

Daniel lowered his head and brushed her lips with his. "I only know God has truly blessed me with your love."

"And our attempts at playing Cupid have ended in happiness for everyone," Patty added. Just as Daniel was about to kiss her again, she frowned and said, "Except Auggie. Daniel—"

"No, Patty," he replied hurriedly. "Augustus must find his own love, when he is ready."

"But you are so accomplished in your role of Cupid, my love," Patty assured the vicar as she drew his head lower for another kiss.